MW01152641

Stuffed

A NOVEL BY

Robert M. Davis

Stuffed

ISBN: 978-1-61170-311-5

Cover designed and illustrated by Bob Archibald.

Published by:

Printed in the USA and UK on acid-free paper.

Also by Robert M. Davis:

The Ticker
Will to Kill
The Crackerjack

To purchase books go to:

amazon.com
barnesandnoble.com
www.rp-author.com/robertdavis

Dedication

To the Rose Family for all of their wonderful support
Howard, Leslie, Debby, and Mike

Chapter One (1958 Thanksgiving Eve)

As soon as Elizabeth opened the restaurant door, she was hit with a mouthwatering aroma and apprehension. She admired oil paintings of the Golden Gate Bridge, Fisherman's Wharf, and other San Francisco tourist attractions hanging on the lobby walls. Mr. B's was mainly patronized by rich, famous, and well-connected clientele, not a twenty-eight-year-old underpaid city librarian who was more apt to eat at Doggie Diner.

A peek into the dining area found tuxedoed waiters serving patrons clad in their finest. Glittery chandeliers offered soft, appetizing illumination as a violinist weaved from one party to the next. She smoothed her J.C. Penney Department Store flower print dress, feeling like a pair of worn white pumps marching into a world of elegant stiletto heels.

"Good evening." The smiling raven-haired hostess was dressed in a stylish green gown and stiletto heels. "Welcome to Mr. B's. Your reservation is under what name?"

"I'm not sure if my fiancé made a reservation," Elizabeth said. "He called me this afternoon at my workplace and asked that I meet him here tonight."

"I see," the hostess said, minus the smile. "Unless your fiancé is Mayor Christopher or columnist Herb Caen, we are booked solid for the next six months. Perhaps you would like to wait for him in our cocktail lounge."

Elizabeth was seated at a small round table in the dimly lit lounge. She shifted several times in the chair, failing to get comfortable. A flickering candle encased in a glass lantern was centered on the tabletop. Clouds of cigarette smoke hovered over the room. A lone male wearing a blue suit occupied a stool at the bar. Behind the bartender, who was sporting a handlebar mustache, backlit shelf lighting showcased different brands of liquor bottles like soldiers lined up for inspection. At the far end of the room, two couples engaged in friendly social banter. Isolated in a middle row, an attractive twosome locked eyes with their hands joined in the middle of the table. A man with striking silver hair sat at the table next to Elizabeth and stared at a dainty sherry glass in front of the empty seat across from him. An "I LIKE IKE" button was fastened to his double-breasted brown suit jacket. Two years from now, Elizabeth would be nearing thirty years of age and Dwight D. Eisenhower will have fulfilled a second and last term as President of the United States.

A cocktail waitress wearing a dark skirt, white blouse, and a black crossover bow tie hustled to the table. Elizabeth clutched her purse. Only two items in her wallet had value: a Texaco gas credit card and maybe enough loose change to purchase a ginger ale.

"Hi, I'm Brandi," the waitress said. "What can I get you from the bar?"

"I think I will wait until my fiancé arrives before ordering a drink," Elizabeth said, peering up at the drink runner with a bogus smile. "He should be here soon."

"The gentleman sitting at the bar would like to buy you a drink." Brandi aimed her tray at the older man in the blue suit. He winked, pointed at Elizabeth, and then at his chest.

Elizabeth emitted a low growl. This wasn't the way she envisioned her big evening out. Her fiancé was late, leaving her un-chaperoned for a middle-aged stranger to try to pick her up. She raised her left hand adorned with the engagement ring she rarely wore in public and wiggled her fingers at Wally the Wolf in creep's clothing.

"Please give the gentleman my thanks, but no thanks," Elizabeth said. "Then warn him my fiancé will be joining me soon. He has an uncontrollable temper, along with black belts in judo, karate, jujitsu, and kick-butt-su."

Elizabeth ran a fingertip over the ring's small diamond. The only black belt her fiancé owned was made from leather, but the waitress looked impressed. So did the man in the blue suit after the waitress whispered in his ear to convey Elizabeth's message. He erased the smile from his lips and motioned to the bartender to refill his glass.

"Pardon me, miss." The silver-haired man turned to face Elizabeth. Tiny wrinkles cornered his blue eyes above a ruddy complexion and set of dimples. "Your sense of humor may have been lost on the waitress and the chap sitting at the bar, but I found it most entertaining." He lifted his chin. "Far be it for me to be an unsolicited Dear Abby advice expert, but if I may, I'd like to offer you another perspective."

Elizabeth frowned. Was the word "perspective" an older generation's way of conveying an opinion? Or was this another flirt technique? She eyed him carefully. At least he had been courteous about asking if he could propose his viewpoint, unlike the man in the blue suit. She motioned her consent with an open palm gesture.

"A pretty young lady shouldn't get annoyed by a man's flirt. Honestly, Liz Taylor would be envious of your exquisite green eyes. Take offense when they stop flirting."

Elizabeth's cheeks warmed. She expected a different response. In a nice way, this gentleman's compliment insinuated she could be a contestant in a Miss Stuck-up pageant.

"Thank you for the flattering remark and counsel," she said. "Believe it or not, this is the first time I have been in a bar unescorted. I'm not much of a drinker, and I haven't worn this much makeup since my high school senior prom."

"I'm sure you will feel much more at ease once your fiancé arrives."

"If he arrives." She glanced at her wristwatch. "I don't even know why he asked me to meet him here. Neither one of us can afford an expensive restaurant like Mr. B's."

"Perhaps your fiancé's intention is to celebrate special news with the person he loves."

Or could it be the opposite? Heaviness seized Elizabeth's chest, a condition she had been battling for the last three years. Did her fiancé request meeting at this classy place so he could break off their engagement like they do in the movies? Or had the past finally caught up with her? Several deep breaths didn't calm the angst surging through her.

"How often do you and your wife come to Mr. B's?" Elizabeth asked, noting the man's wedding band as well as the full glass in front of the vacant chair at his table.

"Once a year to celebrate our anniversary."

"How romantic," she said. "Happy anniversary. Are you also waiting for her to arrive?"

"Margaret won't be joining me tonight or any other night." His Adam's apple jutted in and out. "She's in heaven. I still come to Mr. B's on our anniversary to honor her and our life together. A glass of sherry was her favorite. She wasn't much of a drinker, either."

"I'm so sorry." Elizabeth placed a hand over her heart. "Forgive me for assuming—"

"Please, don't be sorry. I'm a fortunate man. We had forty-six years of marital bliss. How many couples can say that? I wish similar happiness for you and your fiancé, Miss..."

"Please, call me Elizabeth."

"It is nice to meet you, Elizabeth." She accepted his hand. "I'm Holy."

She blinked twice. "Are you a religious man? Or is your given name really Holy?"

"Both."

"I have never met anyone named Holy. Do you have brothers and sisters?"

"Seven brothers."

"I can hardly wait to hear what your parents named them," she said.

"I'm the oldest. In order of birth, there's Jim, Bill, Bob, Ken, John, Tom, and Fred."

"Those are common first names." She patted the side of her brunette bouffant hairdo stiff from hairspray. "Why did your parents name you Holy?"

"Beats the heck out of me." A smile made his dimples spread. "They never told me, and I never asked. But having the name Holy has made me feel special my whole life."

Elizabeth muffled a giggle with her hand, melting much of her trepidation. The gleam in Holy's blue eyes revealed she wasn't the first person to question his unique name. The hostess in the green gown entered the lounge, breezed past blue suit at the bar, and came directly to their tables. She nodded to Holy on her right, but her eyes set on Elizabeth.

"Your fiancé just called, Miss Harper. He said he was very sorry, but he's going to be much later than expected and will get here as soon as possible."

"Thank you." Elizabeth waited for the hostess to depart. "It looks like you will have to put up with me for a bit longer, Holy."

"The pleasure is all mine. However, I'm looking forward to meeting your fiancé."

She settled into the chair sensing this reassuring man was seated next to her for a reason.

"Do you mind if I ask you what your last name is, Holy?"

"I don't mind at all." He sipped his drink.

She waited for Holy's answer. His features remained fixed. Was he a famous San Francisco person she should have recognized? Could he be an underworld boss? Or a Russian spy? What if he was Mr. B, the owner of the restaurant?

"You're reluctant to tell me your last name," she said. "It was rude of me to ask."

"It wasn't rude of you at all, Elizabeth. I want you to guess."

"You want me to guess? There must be a zillion last names." A clip-on earring came off in her hand. She reattached it to her ear. "How can I possibly guess the correct one?"

"I'm told my last name goes very well with my first name," Holy said. "Tell you what. If you say my last name, dinner for you and your fiancé will be my pre-Thanksgiving treat."

"I don't celebrate Thanksgiving, but that is a really sweet offer." Elizabeth twisted her engagement ring. "Okay, I'll play until my fiancé arrives. Is your last name…Mackerel?"

"Holy Mackerel. No, but that's a good start."

"How about Holy Cow?"

"In some countries cows are holy, but Cow isn't my last name."

"Are you Holy Moses?"

"My last name isn't Moses, although I have it on good authority he was a fine fellow."

A tall blonde woman strolled into the cocktail lounge holding onto her date's arm. He was six inches shorter and sported a milk chocolate-colored toupee that looked as if it could melt under a hot California sun. She pulled the man to a stop, squinted, leaned her head forward, and aimed a white-gloved index finger at Elizabeth. There was no mistaking that hooked nose.

"Holy shit!" Elizabeth's fingers went to her mouth, embarrassed about cursing in public. Her good feeling evaporated like steam in the wind. Holy shit.

"Uh, no," Holy said, "my last name isn't...are you all right, Elizabeth? From your troubled expression, one would think Bela Lugosi just arrived in his Dracula costume."

"If I had a choice," Elizabeth said, trembling, "I would choose Dracula rather than the person stuffed in a tight navy blue evening gown and leering at me with her mouth open."

Elizabeth continued to engage in a glare-off with the blonde. They were like two boxers snorting hostility from their respective corners before the opening bell. The blonde abandoned her date and charged to Elizabeth's table.

"Well, I'll be a monkey's aunt." The blonde stopped a yard away from Elizabeth and put her hands on her hips. "If it isn't Betsy Harper."

"Betsy?" Holy said. "Pardon me, Miss, but you are terribly mistaken. This young lady's name isn't Betsy."

"No. She's right, Holy. Betsy is my nickname. I changed to my given name Elizabeth after I moved to San Francisco. The person blocking my view is Sally."

"I never expected to see you again, Betsy," Sally said. "And I'm utterly surprised you have the nerve to show your face in public, especially in a posh place like Mr. B's. Aren't you out of uniform? Shouldn't you be wearing a black and white striped dress with numbers on the back?"

All eyes centered on the two women. The bartender dropped a towel and moved to the side of the bar, ready to break up a catfight. Blue suit was grinning like a tomcat in heat.

"Miss Sally," Holy said in a stern voice. "With all due respect, you are making an unnecessary and unpleasant scene. You have said your piece. My friend Elizabeth, as well as myself, would appreciate you taking your act somewhere else."

Elizabeth gazed at the area above Holy's head. Maybe only archangels could see the halos of fellow guardian angels.

"Tonight is Thanksgiving eve." Sally's fingers made a snap sound as her eyes zoned in on Holy. "For Betsy, it's like being exposed to a full moon before turning into a werewolf-ette. Mister, if you value your life, you should be careful. Very, very careful."

Sally turned and hurried back to her dumbstruck date. "Come on, Herbert. Let's wait for our table in the lobby where there is a better class of people."

"My name is Harold, damn it." Sally's date adjusted his toupee. "Just once, I'd like to find a blonde who isn't brainless. It has to be the bleach."

Elizabeth put her hands together to stop the shaking as Sally and date vacated the lounge.

"Of all people to run into, Sally is the last person I would want to see," Elizabeth said.

Holy placed a round coaster in front of her that had a black top hat and "Mr. B's" imprinted on it. Then he positioned the glass of sherry on the coaster.

"I don't think Margaret would mind sharing her drink with you," he said. "Sally acted as if you committed a nefarious crime. I find that hard to believe. What did you do, steal her boyfriend? Take her place on the cheerleading squad? Catch her cheating on an exam?"

"Murder!" Mascara-stained tears streamed down Elizabeth's cheeks. "My action led to the first homicide case in our town's history."

"You took part in a murder, Elizabeth?" The volume in Holy's voice increased.

"If only we could take hidden shames buried in our psyche closets and have them dry cleaned." Elizabeth dabbed her face with a handkerchief from her purse. "I have feared this moment would come. Now that it has happened, I'm unprepared."

"You said you were involved in a homicide." Holy patted her hand. "That doesn't mean you actually committed a murder, does it? Perhaps, metaphorically, you aided and abetted in a homicide by holding a gun while someone else pulled the trigger. Or maybe you were guilty by association and unwittingly involved in a crime. Or could it be you simply observed a murder and the traumatic experience made you feel involved."

"I wish it was that simple." She gulped for air and sniffed several times. "Sally and I both lived in a small town called Bobsville. You probably haven't heard of it. It's near the Nevada border. It's a sweet little community – or at least it was to me. My parents moved to Bobsville after I graduated from college, and I was lucky enough to get a job there as a librarian. Really, it was such a pleasant place to live. But then something happened. No, that's not right. I made it sound like an earthquake or a tornado occurred. No, I made a choice and decided to take part in something with Sally's roommate, Paige, which turned into a terrible, terrible scheme. Have you ever experienced evil before, Holy? I never did until three Thanksgivings ago. Evil can pretend to be something else, even working for good. The only way I can explain is to tell the whole story from the beginning. Three years ago, five of us united to teach a young man named Slayter Jones a lesson for his own good after he scheduled three Thanksgiving dinners with three women in the same day..."

Chapter Two (1955 Thanksgiving Day)

Right on cue, Slayter's stomach expressed its hurt feelings by belting out an aria of gross eruptions. Dr. Sinn's unkempt gray eyebrows jutted into a furrowed forehead like he could decipher intestine-ese. Slayter placed a palm on his abdomen trying to determine if the intense pressure in his gut had pushed an innie bellybutton into an outie.

"I feel sicker than a Chihuahua suffering from Montezuma's Revenge," Slayter said.

"Frankly, Mr. Jones, you don't look so hot either," Dr. Sinn replied.

Slayter's gurgling belly voiced its sentiments again. Most likely his stinging dark brown eyes were inundated with bloodshot streaks. He noted several diplomas hanging on the wall certifying Goodwin Axel Sinn as a medical doctor. Maybe Dr. Sinn flunked bedside manner in medical school? Did they even teach bedside manner fifty years ago?

The spectacled physician lifted the stethoscope dangling from his neck and placed it on the examination room counter. He removed a pipe from the pocket of his white smock, raised it to his lips, struck a wood match on the sole of a brown wingtip Oxford, and held the flame over the pipe bowl until the tobacco embers turned red. His mouth formed into an oval before blowing out a series of smoke ring clouds.

The pungent odor drifted down to Slayter's nauseated stomach. He grabbed the current 1955 November magazine issue of *Modern Doctor Confessions* from a wall rack and waved the haze to an open window screen before he lost his Oreos again. Clearly, Dr. Sinn didn't believe the latest reports about smoking being harmful to one's health.

"Who is your Bobsville family physician?" Dr. Sinn stroked loose skin under his chin.

"Dr. Tyme. I was hoping he would be on duty tonight."

"Justin Tyme is a fine physician. I'm not married and have no children, so I volunteered to take his on-call duties, in part so he could enjoy his family's Thanksgiving festivities."

"Bobsville is a small town," Slayter said. "If you whisper something in a public john, it's radioactive gossip on the main drag before the water goes down. Yet I don't recall ever seeing you or even hearing about you."

"I moved to Bobsville a few months ago. You see, I often relocate from one town to another, wherever my services are needed. Plus, I have a grand-niece that lives here."

Slayter flinched after a lightning bolt lit up the night, followed by a rumble and crack of thunder. Another layer of his frayed nerves peeled away. Rhythmic raindrops thumped the roof, adding one more concern for him to endure. Did he forget to roll up his driver's side window? A searing pain traveled from the epicenter of his stomach up to his head. Right now, sitting in a cold puddle was the least of his worries. His eyes watered. He gazed at the stethoscope resting on the counter, along with jars of tongue depressors, cotton swabs, and un-inflated rainbow-colored balloons waiting to come to life with puffs of hot air.

"The ache in my empty stomach has gotten progressively worse," Slayter said. "A family's guest bathroom will never be the same due to whatever sickness I've got."

"Actually, Mr. Jones, I'm amazed you aren't in worse condition."

"It has to be the flu or a bad case of food poisoning, right?" Slayter expelled a belch that brought on ringing in his left ear. A new symptom he could add to a rapidly growing list. "How many other patients have come down with what I'm suffering from?"

"I can say with conviction you are the only person in Bobsville who has the ailment you are experiencing. However, considering you consumed three Thanksgiving dinners today with three different women in three locations, food poisoning is a logical assumption on your part." Dr. Sinn puffed out more smoke rings. "Logical but false. The food itself didn't bring on your symptoms."

"Then what is making my stomach feel like a volcano ready to spew hot lava? Again." Slayter ran a hand through his short, sandy-colored hair, messing up his part. "Hold on, doc. How can you be so sure it isn't food poisoning or flu when you haven't examined me? What's more, how did you know I attended three Thanksgiving dinners today?"

Dr. Sinn produced a toothy smile. The popular toothpaste commercial jingle, "*You'll wonder where the yellow went when you brush your teeth with Pepsodent,*" played in Slayter's head. He should probably keep that little toothpaste dental ditty to himself.

"My diagnosis is correct," Dr. Sinn said. "There is no need for me to do an exam since I know what you are suffering from." He adjusted his glasses with a forefinger. "Your Thanksgiving meals were basted with bitterness, along with several noxious ingredients I created for the hostesses to put into your food to produce the symptoms you are feeling."

Was this doctor from Realsville? Slayter's nerves jumped to red alert status. His twenty-five-year-old lips twitched like a ninety-year-old man with a neurological disorder. He squeezed his eyes shut. If he was in the midst of a grisly nightmare, now would be a good time for him to wake up. His eyelids opened, blinking an SOS coded message like a damaged ship at sea. Damn. It wasn't a dream, but he was experiencing a real nightmare.

"You're a medical doctor, for criminy sakes." Slayter rolled the magazine into a baton and aimed it at Dr. Sinn. "You took a hypocritical oath to save patients, not poison them."

"Your point is well taken, Mr. Jones. Yet, would I be a hypocrite if my patient didn't deserve to be saved?" The doctor shrugged his bony shoulders. "For what it's worth, my intentions are honorable. Just because my last name is Sinn, it doesn't make me sinister."

Slayter's pulse quickened. Even in his weakened condition, he could beat the snot out of Dr. Sinn. So could an anorexic Girl Scout, but that didn't stop him from fearing this man.

"Even though we've never met before," Slayter said, "for some reason I make your chemicals boil. Why would you take part in such an evil plot? It doesn't make sense."

"I fully understand why you would feel that way. Your behavior is a result of your environment, Mr. Jones." Dr. Sinn's voice remained unemotional and calm. "Put another way, you are a person who keeps trying to win life's lottery without ever buying a ticket."

"What the heck is that supposed to mean? I've never played a lottery or an Irish Sweepstakes ticket in my life."

"A metaphor, Mr. Jones." Dr. Sinn aimed his pipe stem at Slayter as if it was a loaded pistol. "You are a person endowed with all-American boy good looks, high intelligence, and many untapped natural talents. In spite of your abilities, you have been enabled by family, friends, and townspeople your whole life. I was told you were voted 'Most Likely to Succeed Without Ever Trying' in high school. You have selfishly taken advantage of anyone willing to perform the tasks you should have been doing for yourself. In essence, you use people as shortcuts."

"You make it sound like I'm a bad person." Slayter waved away another smoke cloud. "Ever since I was a child, people have treated me with excessive kindness. What you are failing to comprehend, Dr. Sinn, is that the individuals who assist me get more joy out of it than I do. I'm actually doing them a favor. I'd be taking away all of their pleasure if I were to change my ways."

"Are you doing your older brother Warren any *favors* by allowing him to let you live room and board free in his house? Are you doing Warren a *favor* by accepting a monthly allowance from him? Are you doing Rhoda, your newlywed sister-in-law, a *favor* while she cooks and cleans for you?"

"Wait," Slayter said, "how do you know all this? And, well, no, I wouldn't exactly call those *favors*. But isn't it clear to you, if I wasn't living in my brother's house, Rhoda would still be cleaning and cooking? What's more, I do supplement my income as a golf instructor at Bobsville's Municipal Golf Course whenever the pro has a hangover from the night before. Warren's generosity allows me the opportunity to finish the novel I'm working on."

"Right, you fancy yourself as an author. I believe your novel is called *What For*."

"This is getting creepy. How do you know all of this? And the title is *What If?*."

"Whatever," Dr. Sinn responded. "The main point is Paige

Turner, the literary editor your brother Warren is paying for, is also writing the story for you."

As bad as that sounded, it was a correct statement. Slayter stomped a desert boot into the linoleum floor, then he placed a hand on his stomach. He was narrating the story that had been in his head for years to Paige to transcribe his words into a novel. The process made perfect sense to him. After all, why should he go to the trouble of learning how to craft a novel when an editor could simply type the words of his story for him?

"What's more," Dr. Sinn continued, "are you doing your librarian friend Betsy any *favors* by allowing her to do all of the research on the novel?"

"Listen, Betsy is my best friend. She volunteered. I didn't even have to ask her. Think about it, who is better at doing research than a librarian?" Slayter put a hand over his mouth to suppress another belch. "It's really irritating that you have been here a few months and I've never heard of you, yet you seem to know lots of things about me – even if they are incorrect."

"What you fail to recognize, Mr. Jones, is that the amusement you believe your supporters receive has not done them or *you* any favors – just the opposite, in fact." Dr. Sinn picked up a little hammer used to test patient reflexes and tapped it into his palm. "There is a difference between helping someone in need and enabling a person. How do you expect to grow as a man if you don't experience life's challenges on your own? What would happen if you had to fend for yourself without depending on other people?"

"A difficult question for me to answer." Slayter squeezed his hands together to counter a sharp pang in his stomach. "I don't remember a time when folks haven't assisted me."

"Until today, Mr. Jones. Until today."

"Is that some kind of threat? I just pleaded guilty to a non-capital offense of empowering others to do whatever I needed to get done. What other crimes did I commit to induce the wrath of family, friends, and a deranged family physician?"

"Allow me to enlighten you, Mr. Jones. You deceived all three of your Thanksgiving hostesses today into believing you would spend time solely with them."

"Correct, but deception wasn't my intention. I didn't want to hurt anyone's feelings by turning them down, so I accepted their invitations and then figured out a way to pull it off. How could that be a major transgression and reason to poison me?"

Dr. Sinn performed a *tsk-tsk* sound with his tongue the way a parent would treat a mischievous child. He ogled a framed black and white photo from yesteryear of a curly-haired young woman with a nose that dominated her thin face. He then turned back to Slayter, removed his glasses, and wiped his eyes.

"You questioned how I know so much about you and why I would involve myself in this type of matter." Dr. Sinn placed his glasses back onto his nose crooked. "After medical school, I planned to marry the young lady in the photo. She ran off with a Romeo and never came back. Ever since then, I have made a hobby of teaching rogues who takes advantage of vulnerable women a lesson for their own benefit. Scoundrels exactly like you, Mr. Jones."

"Just my luck you didn't take up collecting stamps as a hobby. Instead, you hire out as a contract poison assassin."

"I prefer to be identified as a rogue equalizer by righting the wrongs of individuals who take advantage of others." Dr. Sinn puffed out a mass of smoke that made Slayter cough and then placed his pipe on the counter. "Mr. Jones, are you denying you pulled on the vulnerable heartstrings of each Thanksgiving hostess by toying shamefully with their affections? Isn't that the real reason you didn't want them to know about each other?"

"You're way off base. Again, I was only trying to avoid hurting their feelings. I don't know where you got your info, but it's false. I never deceived any of them romantically. In essence, you are condemning and convicting an innocent man without a trial."

"Then why did four individuals, including each Thanksgiving hostess, seek me out and request that I make you realize just how appalling your behavior has been? I heard narratives about how you pressured, many times, one of the hostesses to share her bed with you. How you made constant improper advances to a married woman. And how you misled a naïve young lady into believing you were in love with her."

"You can't be serious? Those are out-and-out lies." Slayter scrunched the front of his shirt into a knot. "I need to know. Is the concoction you created for the hostesses lethal?"

"Is your will up to date?" Dr. Sinn replied.

"My will?" Slayter thought his heart would break through his chest. "Wills are for folks who have money and assets – neither of which I have."

"As it happens, you do have one very shaky asset, Mr. Jones."

"And what would that be?"

"Your life," Dr. Sinn announced.

Slayter peered up at the ceiling's spinning light fixture fan that wasn't in operation. Dr. Sinn just foreshadowed his chance of survival to be as good as bringing beef jerky back to life. How did he get himself into this situation? What was more important, how could he get out of it? His face leaned towards the window screen to suck in as much air as possible. Then he focused on the doctor's unsympathetic eyes and realized two things. He was in some deep doo-doo without a plunger, and most likely he wasn't going to receive a balloon for being a good patient.

"I wish I could write myself out of this one," Slayter grumbled.

"On that note," Dr. Sinn said, sharpening the tone of his dull voice, "if I give you a chance to rewrite your own inevitable ending, would you be interested?"

Chapter Three (1955 Thanksgiving Day)

Bubbles of sweat primed Slayter's neck as if he was the defendant in a court of law anxious to learn his fate from a judge's decision. Of course he was interested in amending his situation after ingesting tainted Thanksgiving food, but at what cost? Selling his soul to this devil doctor?

Heavy raindrops continued to pelt the examination room roof, masking noises produced by Slayter's gurgling stomach. Dr. Sinn placed the pipe stem between his lips and tapped four fingers on the counter waiting for Slayter to respond to his rhetorical question.

A neighborhood dog launched into a barking fit after another thunderclap. Slayter was tempted to bark back. He had been targeted by five angry people to be the Thanksgiving entrée of a well-organized revenge scheme. The only difference between Slayter's situation and Tom Turkey: in Tom's case, it wasn't personal. Why would once loyal family and friends turn against him by painting corrupted pictures to a hired hit man who poisons his prey as a pastime?

"What do I have to do to survive without becoming as incoherent as a kumquat?" Slayter said in a hoarse voice that sounded like it came from a stranger.

"Follow me, Mr. Jones." The chair, or was it Dr. Sinn, creaked when he rose to his feet.

"You want me to follow you?" Slayter stared at the back of Dr. Sinn's gray head as he neared the doorway. "Follow you where?"

"The way I see it, at the moment, your chances are slim to none and your only friend Slim has just put his house up for sale. What more do you have to lose by following me?"

Another loaded question. Slayter didn't move a muscle. His first inclination had been to run for help rather than follow the doctor. Then again, Dr. Sinn had offered him a chance to alter his own inevitable ending. Was it a trick to steer Slayter away from fleeing so the doctor could lead him into a far worse situation rather than opening survival's door? How much worse can it get? Slayter put his head into his hands. The hi-fi in his brain was spinning a 33 1/3 LP record at 45 RPM speed, garbling his logical thinking. One way or another, he'd have to roll the dice and make a decision that wouldn't make him crap out.

Slayter wobbled to his feet. He blinked away red and yellow floaters. His arms extended to regain balance. He took a second look at the framed black and white photograph of the young woman who had been Dr. Sinn's ladylove from long ago, before a Don Juan romanced her away, leading the young medical student down a path of lifetime retribution. For an instant, Slayter felt a smidgen sorry for the poor old guy.

Even in his weakened condition, Slayter caught up with the doctor in the hallway. He needed to create a game plan. What had he learned thus far? Not a heck of a lot. Dr. Sinn was jilted as a young man and never got over it. The doctor was new to Bobsville, had a niece here, and volunteered to take Dr. Tyme's on-call duties knowing a hurting Slayter would come to his office for medical attention. This wasn't Dr. Sinn's debut poison party. How many victims had the doctor previously poisoned? How many of those sufferers were still around to talk about it? Clearly the three Thanksgiving hostesses were the poisoners, making him the poisonee, but he was still clueless as to why. Also, Dr. Sinn had said four people approached him. Who was the fifth conspirator?

Slayter trailed Dr. Sinn into a room that resembled a laboratory. He cupped a hand over his eyebrows to shield bright overhead lights. Dr. Sinn positioned himself behind a counter centered in the middle. Test tubes, chemicals, and an interconnected glass cylinder contraption resembling a miniature amusement park rollercoaster ride were situated on the Formica top. A station in the corner had a microscope and scientific equipment whose functions were way beyond Slayter's comprehension. Every inch of shelf space housed weighty tomes, chemicals with scientific names, and large jars containing weird-looking objects floating in a lime-green solution that reminded him of his high school biology classroom. He was grateful his medium-sized body wouldn't fit into any of the jars.

Dr. Sinn lifted a glass chemical stirrer and motioned like an orchestra conductor for Slayter to sit in a chair fronting the counter. Slayter plopped down onto the seat. The shiny metal cabinets supporting the countertop reflected his sickly complexion and bloodshot brown eyes. He hardly recognized the person staring back at him, but at least he was still breathing. If Dr. Sinn created doses of poison specifically for him, it made sense the doctor would also make an antidote to counteract the poison. Slayter frantically searched for labels worded with "antidote," "new," "improved," and "longer lasting."

"Okay, I followed you here," Slayter said. "What do I have to do to secure a remedy that will offset the poison I ingested?"

"Ultimately, find the person who has the antidote."

"Wait!" Slayter jumped up. Bad move. One hand went to his stomach, the other to his head. He fell back into the chair. "You don't have the antidote? What kind of game—"

Dr. Sinn repeatedly tapped the stirrer on the countertop until Slayter quieted.

"Calm down, Mr. Jones. I created an antidote. Your mission? You have three hours - give or take a few minutes - to find the person who has the antidote and convince him or her to hand it over to you. Now if you remain seated and agree to all my conditions, I will mix a solution to relieve the symptoms you are now experiencing."

"I agree to any and all of your conditions," Slayter replied. "Start mixing, doc."

"Not so fast. That sounded more like a premature exclamation rather than a sincere verbal agreement. Consider the situation you are in as a real-life TV soap opera akin to *Search for Tomorrow*. Only in this drama, there might not be a tomorrow to search for unless I'm convinced you will follow the conditions you agree to. Is that understood?"

"I get it." Slayter tried to blow out the hurt from his stomach. "You are saying my butt is destined for a six-foot rut if I renege. I can't believe this is happening to me. If that was condition number one, I agree. Can we please hurry the condition part along?"

"The first condition: if you physically harm me, you can kiss your antidote goodbye."

"Agreed," Slayter said. "What is the next condition?"

"The second condition: no one can assist you in your quest to find the antidote." Dr. Sinn ran his tongue over his lower lip. "I wonder how receptive your enablers will be to converse with you since they are the same individuals you have used and abused."

Slayter panted out breaths as if he had run a marathon. Dr. Sinn was forcing him to go on an antidote scavenger hunt all alone. If that wasn't difficult enough, he only had three hours to find the cure. Then he would need to persuade the person holding the antidote he was worthy of being saved. An impossible task in his condition, unless he could get someone to help him, which would be a deal breaker. Dr. Sinn had stacked the chemical deck against him. What if he went straight to the police? They could make the doctor prepare another batch of antidote, then lock him up in a loony bin where he belonged.

"Condition number three: you are not permitted to contact the police."

Slayter held back a smile. Unwittingly, Dr. Sinn just gave him the opening he had been looking for. How would the doctor know if he went to the police for help?

"I expect you to be on the honor system," Dr. Sinn said. "However, in case you are unable to honor my system, you will be followed everywhere you go by someone with a two-way walkie-talkie radio detailing your every move back to me. Furthermore, each member of the poison party is waiting for my call. If I tell them you broke our agreement, they will not interact with you. Do I make myself clear, Mr. Jones?"

"Damn," Slayter muttered. Did Dr. Sinn have the ability to read his mind? There had to be another way to overcome the predicament he was in. Condition number three didn't state another person representing Slayter couldn't contact the police. Maybe he could ditch the walkie-talkie person for a short time and find someone to help him. But who could he trust? Obviously, the three Thanksgiving hostesses were on the other team.

Slayter massaged the back of his neck. He could always count on Warren, his older brother. Warren never denied Slayter anything, including allowing him to continue living at the house without paying rent even after his sister-in-law Rhoda moved in. Since Slayter was a scratch golfer without practicing, Warren had formed a group of buddies to financially back his younger brother to pursue a career on the pro golf circuit. Slayter refused the offer. Going pro would have eliminated the joy of playing golf and put a damper on his passion to launch the novel anchored in his head. It also would have meant his sponsors would be reliant on Slayter to make a profitable return on their investment, rather than Slayter being dependent on them. Warren never shied away from being in his corner. His brother would be the perfect person to assist him in his time of need. Slayter picked at a cuticle on his thumb. Then again, Warren was also married to the woman who was the first hostess to poison him. Whose side would Warren be on?

Slayter shuddered at the thought of Warren being in cahoots with the hostesses and Dr. Sinn. An idiotic thought, but there had to be someone else who would, without a doubt, assist him just in case his thought wasn't so foolish. The image of marionette Howdy Doody's face floated in his head. His childhood friend, Doody, was unblessed with red hair, freckles, and a goofy grin just like Howdy. Doody would do anything Slayter asked, with no strings attached. Mentally, the only difference between Doody and the end of late night TV programming was sometimes Doody's Test Pattern didn't come on. But Doody had been Slayter's loyal lapdog pal since they were in grade school. Contacting Doody seemed like a good plan, since it was the only strategy Slayter could come up with.

"Are you paying attention to me, Mr. Jones?" Dr. Sinn asked in an annoyed tone.

"Absolutely. Every word. Are there any other conditions I need to agree to?"

"The fourth condition is a forewarning: There isn't a doctor in Bobsville who can help you, except for me. The nearest hospital is over sixty miles away. Plus, the probability of creating an antidote in the time you have left is not in your favor. The best chance you have is based on *your* ability to obey my conditions. *Your* ability to locate the individual who has the antidote, and *your* ability to convince that person to forgive you and hand it over. In other words, the only person you can rely on, Mr. Jones, is *yourself*."

"Do you get your jollies by inflicting pain? How much do you charge for your services?"

"Not one red cent - not that I have ever seen a red penny - but I do take donations of gratitude so I can continue dealing with individuals like yourself."

"This is unbelievable." Slayter fired back. "Do you advertise in the yellow pages?"

"I don't have to. Word of mouth is quite effective."

"Have Poison – Will Make House Calls."

"That's one way of putting it. Any other questions, Mr. Jones?"

"Will you at least tell me who the fourth person is? And who has the antidote?"

"If I provide answers to those questions, I'd be enabling you." Dr. Sinn revealed a pocket watch on a chain. "Time is your main asset and a major obstacle. What is your decision?"

"You leave me no choice but to agree to all of your conditions."

"A wise decision, Mr. Jones." Dr. Sinn squeezed open an envelope and peeked at the contents. "It should only take a few minutes for the powder to fully activate, then you'll have three hours to find the person holding your antidote that is also in powder form."

"Please hurry." Slayter clenched his fists. "I'm in a world of hurt here, doc."

Slayter rocked back and forth to combat increasing discomfort. He had a host of other questions, but it would be counterproductive to divert Dr. Sinn's attention while mixing chemicals. Sometime soon he would need to discover how the concept to poison him got started. Who was the leader that turned everyone against him? How did Dr. Sinn get involved? Was there really an antidote, or was he being sent on a wild turkey chase?

The doctor lifted a skinny-necked vial containing a clear liquid and filled a drinking glass. He jiggled the envelope, tipped it towards the glass until bluish-green particles escaped into the fluid. A small portion fell to the floor. Slayter's mouth salivated for the loose powder. Dr. Sinn mixed the contents with the glass stirrer. The concoction hissed and fizzed. If the drinking glass cracked or melted, all bets were off.

"Is that stuff supposed to make me feel better or put me out of my misery?"

"There's only one way to find out. It should be ready in another minute."

Dr. Sinn held the glass up to the light and studied the contents. There wasn't a clock in the room, but Slayter heard ticking. This could be the longest or shortest minute in his life. He looked at one of the creatures in the lime-green solution on the shelf and closed his eyes. His eyelids lifted when the doctor handed him the glass. Would he rather jump off a cliff into raging waters filled with hungry sharks, alligators, and snakes; play Russian roulette with a fully loaded gun; or drink the solution?

"Bottoms up, Mr. Jones," Dr. Sinn said. "It would behoove you to drink every last drop."

Slayter studied the solution. Some particles hadn't dissolved. It was nitty-gritty time. The odor was distinct, reminding him of a number of different spices and herbs. He sucked in a deep breath. Would the remedy help him temporarily or not? He blew out the air he was holding and gulped the contents down like a thirsty desert nomad. It tasted like a spicy vegetable fizzing bromide. He squeezed the glass and waited for his destiny. His stomach made an eerie noise he had never heard before, followed by a dynamic belch powerful enough to shake Dr. Sinn's chemistry glassware like a passing train. Slayter's eyes widened. The discomfort he had been experiencing disappeared, as if he was the subject of a Harry Houdini magic act. He placed the glass onto the floor, touched his stomach, then his head, and smiled as if he never had been poisoned. Dr. Sinn could make a fortune out of poisoning people and selling his extraordinary fixer-elixir.

Dr. Sinn twisted the dial of a kitchen timer to sixty, his way of pointing out Slayter's life-clock was on its first of three hours - give or take a few minutes. Slayter's shoe knocked over the empty glass as he sprinted for the doorway.

Chapter Four (1958 Thanksgiving Eve)

By the time Elizabeth finished sharing the encounter between Dr. Sinn and Slayter Jones, a new crop of lounge lizards had replaced the previous patrons. Even the hound dog in the blue suit departed with his tail between his legs, unaccompanied.

Holy hoisted a hand in the air to catch the waitress' attention and pointed to their empty glasses. Then he turned to Elizabeth with both arms folded across his chest.

"That was quite an amazing and entertaining tale." Holy's eyes widened. "Although your story was quite remarkable, with all due respect, I'm cynical about its validity, with the exception of one thing. Seriously, a young man who was so accustomed to being pampered by family and friends, he never had to do anything for himself since everyone took great pleasure in spoiling him? It kind of reminded me of stories I've read about monarchs born into royalty." Holy produced a modest smile. "Then, unexpectedly, his indulgers revolt against him because he scheduled three Thanksgiving Day dinners with different women. Not only that, what I found even more outrageous, a family doctor who would poison a patient as a lesson in life? Come on Elizabeth, could it be this Slayter Jones chap was telling the truth about not wanting to hurt any feelings? Or the hostesses were jealous of each other and took it out on poor Slayter? Or perhaps the yarn you just spun was meant to pull an old man's leg because you couldn't guess my last name?"

"I don't blame you for being skeptical, Holy." She maneuvered the bottom of the sherry glass to make imaginary circles on the table. "If I hadn't been involved, I probably wouldn't have believed it, either. That being said, you piqued my curiosity. What was the one thing that made you think my story could be true and not fabricated?"

"That blonde woman, Sally. Her response to you and your reaction validated something horrific took place three years ago in your hometown. How does she fit into the picture?"

"Three years ago in Bobsville, Sally was just as tall and a brunette. She had nothing to do with the treachery that took place except being related to Dr. Sinn, but Sally provided the seed of what would transpire. Clearly, she's still resentful, as were many of the townsfolk. It's the reason I moved away and applied for a librarian job in San Francisco."

"Who died?" Holy asked. "Who is the murderer? And who—"

"You sound like an owl, Holy. Believe me, this story is convoluted, and it gets even more complicated. If I tell it to you out of sequence, it will only confuse you more."

"I'm beginning to get that message. You mentioned Slayter's older brother. His name was Warren, right? But you never said anything about their mother and father. Where were their parents during the Thanksgiving Day shenanigans?"

"I was told Slayter was seven years old when his parents were killed in a tragic accident after they pulled into the parking lot of Big Bertha's Bodacious Burgers in Bobsville. Their car's front bumper hit the base of the restaurant's large sign holding up a caricature of Big Bertha, and it fell and crushed them." Elizabeth's voice quivered. "It's hard to imagine how anything like that could happen. Slayter was fortunate his brother Warren was old enough to take on the responsibility of raising him."

"I get it." Holy's blue eyes lit up. "Warren and the people of Bobsville went out of their way to ease the pain of Slayter's loss of his parents, and they never stopped."

"Exactly," Elizabeth said. "As you can see, it got out of hand. In essence, Slayter became a community project. I learned that coeds would do his homework. Teachers ignored his unexcused absences knowing full well he was playing golf. Slayter was the quarterback for his high school football team. His coach would call all of the plays to make it easier for him. What was so crazy, Slayter was perfectly capable of doing whatever needed to get done, but people would automatically do it for him as if it was their duty. Slayter was an A student. He was elected school president without even running. When his football coach got kicked out of a game for arguing, Slayter called all the plays, and the Bobcats routed the other team. He was well equipped to do any task on his own, but why do it when it isn't necessary? For Slayter, it was a bad habit he never considered breaking."

"You are, no doubt, the naïve girl who fell in love with Slayter. How did you meet him?"

"At the library. Slayter strolled in one day and asked the head librarian about research for his novel. She led him to me and whispered, 'You can thank me later.'"

Elizabeth's heart thumped the same way it did when she was first introduced to Slayter.

"The request, itself, wasn't unusual," Elizabeth continued. "As a city librarian, I assisted individuals needing information about certain subjects or books; students seeking material for school projects; or guiding writers on the best way to research their work. At the time, I didn't realize Slayter's definition of help meant I would do all the research for his novel, even though he was capable of doing the task himself. But that didn't stop me from volunteering my services if it meant I could spend more time with him. I stopped seeing the guy I had been dating. After all, what young single gal wouldn't want a smart, charismatic, boyishly handsome man with mesmerizing dark brown eyes, loveable infectious laugh, and only one character flaw?"

"What kind of material did Slayter want you to research for his novel *What If?*"

"*What If?* was about a young man named Hunter who gets knocked out in a college football game. Hunter wakes up with a gift – he can see into the future." Elizabeth's mouth curled into a grin. "Initially, Slayter wanted to find out if the gift to know something will happen before it happens was real. If so, what was it called?"

"Interesting plot. What did you discover besides being immediately attracted to Slayter?"

"That ability to see into the future is real," she said. "It's called precognition. Sometimes it comes in the form of a dream. And I'm not ashamed about falling for Slayter. Countless women had a crush on him. Ladies of all ages blatantly flirted with him. In fact, I initially thought Slayter and his attractive - albeit much older - editor Paige were a twosome. When I asked him if it was okay with Paige that we spend so much time together, he expressed his surprise and said their relationship was strictly business and nothing was going on between them." Elizabeth's eyes narrowed. "I wasn't as naïve as you think, Holy. From the get-go, I was aware of his one negative trait as well as all of the amazing qualities he possessed. It didn't take long for me to learn the extent of how he allowed people to assist him. If I wanted more than a working connection with Slayter, my approach had to be different. So I gave him the impression I wasn't interested in a romantic relationship. We hit it off immediately and became inseparable as the best of platonic friends. I had no doubt in my mind Slayter loved me, he just didn't know it. So I waited patiently for him to get a clue."

"Holy moley!" A man jumped up from kneeling on the lounge floor to embrace his fiancée while she ogled the sparkling engagement ring on her finger. "She said yes!"

The crowd cheered and clapped when the tearful young lady displayed the engagement ring for everyone to see. Elizabeth touched her small diamond again. She was happy for both of them and troubled her fiancé wasn't with her to witness this touching scene.

"I'm a bit confused," Holy said, after the room quieted. "You fell in love with your best friend who conceivably was the beau of your dreams, with the exception of one imperfection. Then you and two other women inexplicably united to poison the poor fella as punishment for scheduling three Thanksgiving dinners. Was it possible this Dr. Jekyll-Sinn character brainwashed the three of you to turn into Miss Hydes so you would take part in a diabolical scheme to kill Slayter Jones?"

Elizabeth shook her head and gave Holy a dismissive hand wave. She would have asked the same questions he fired at her. From Holy's point of view, the outside looking in, it made every person involved look like wicked sinners. As it turned out, they were.

"It will make more sense when I put it into context," Elizabeth said. "Dr. Sinn didn't seek us out, we approached him. It was never our intention to kill Slayter. On the contrary, we wanted to help Slayter – the right way – by teaching him a hard lesson that would show how letting people do everything for him was, in effect, disabling."

"Poison is an extreme way to teach someone a lesson, whether Slayter deserved it or not. Wouldn't it have been wiser as a group to inform him in no uncertain terms his days of being coddled were over and he needed to take responsibility for his own actions?"

"In hindsight, that would have been our best mode of action," she said. "If you can, Holy, please try to put on Slayter Jones' hat for a moment. If you allowed people to help you all of your life, it's all you know. It's what you expect. Do you really think a group of well-meaning folks could verbally persuade you to change your ways?"

"When you present it that way, probably not," Holy said "Nevertheless, I could never sponsor the severe measure of poisoning a person. Certainly, the answer to this conundrum should have been to create a happy medium for all parties."

"That is exactly what we did." Elizabeth clenched her fingers together to make a tight fist. "The poison was bogus. The concoction Dr. Sinn created was a mixture of individual foods and spices that often upset digestive systems. A combination of ingredients like eggplant, lactose, caffeine, peppers, and a whole lot more. It was like adding atomic to bomb. Slayter was led to believe his horrendous stomachache was caused by a deadly poison applied to his Thanksgiving meals and the only way he could survive would be to find the one person who possessed the antidote in three hours without anyone's help. In truth, we weren't privy to which person Dr. Sinn chose to receive the permanent antidote that would relieve his symptoms. Maybe the doctor was fearful someone would spill the tainted beans."

"You mean to tell me there were no toxic components in his food?"

"Just ingredients to give Slayter an agonizing stomachache, excruciating headache, and many other vile symptoms to make him believe he had only a few hours to live."

"Here you go." Brandi removed the empty glasses from the table and placed a sherry in front of Elizabeth and a Scotch and soda for Holy. "Will there be anything else, Mr.— "

"Thank you, Brandi." Holy picked up his drink and gently bumped it against the sherry glass. "Let's see if I have this straight. Slayter was sent on a wild antidote chase in search for a remedy that would counteract poisons that weren't toxic, as punishment for deceiving three women and for taking advantage of people who were kind to him. Women in Bobsville sure take their Thanksgivings seriously, don't they?"

"Of course, I was disappointed he was trying to deceive me, but his deception wasn't the straw that broke the turkey's back. Tainting his food was a vehicle for five individuals with different agendas to open Slayter's eyes and teach him a lesson he would never forget."

"What possible grudge could any of you have had against Slayter to hurt him that much?"

"I can give you five legitimate one-word descriptions: jealousy, greed, revenge, humiliation, and love." Elizabeth waited to compose herself. "It started six days before Thanksgiving when a malicious lie snowballed into a series of lies that led to a tragedy."

Holy's head leaned forward, a gesture that asked her to continue with her story.

"In our attempt to make Slayter aware of his inability to be dependent on himself," she said, "I didn't realize one member of our party really wanted Slayter dead."

Chapter Five (1955 Thanksgiving Day)

Slayter raced away from Dr. Sinn's office and headed to his car parked across the street. The rainstorm had weakened into a heavy mist. A few minutes ago he had been racked in pain and close to expiring. Now he had 180 minutes of reprieve before the solution Dr. Sinn gave him lost its mojo. He sucked in one breath after another of moist evening air, grateful to be alive and amazed about how good he was feeling.

He lifted the collar of his blue sports coat. His ideal life had turned topsy-turvy in one day. What made today's Thanksgiving hostesses - and a person yet to be identified - seek out Dr. Sinn with different grudges that gave false impressions of him, especially after each hostess reiterated the importance of his presence? Newlywed sister-in-law Rhoda was eager to prepare her first Thanksgiving dinner and prove to her husband and brother-in-law she could cook a decent meal. Paige Turner, an editor he hired to transcribe his oral story into typed words, was anxious to meet with him and receive the final chapter to complete her assignment. Betsy, a librarian and his best friend, was excited about him sharing Thanksgiving dinner with her family. He didn't have the heart to disappoint any of them on their special occasions. Did they decide to poison him before or after their invites? What could he have done to make each lady angry enough to want to hurt him?

Both sides of the street were packed with parked cars. Slayter skidded to a stop and straddled a manhole cover in the middle of the road. Which vehicle was harboring Dr. Sinn's spy? A quick look north and south proved futile. Rather than squandering precious time by inspecting each car, it would be more prudent to locate his buddy Doody. He wiped precipitation from his face as he advanced to his faded blue Volkswagen Beetle that he fondly referred to as his Bug on wheels. Sure enough, he had left the driver's side window down. Once again, he envisioned sitting in a puddle of water as he marched to his car berating himself.

"Holy shards!" Tiny pieces of glass on the pavement glistened from the streetlight illumination. "I didn't leave the window open. Someone busted it to pieces."

Glass crunched under his hard rubber-soled desert boots while he examined his car. He didn't have to worry about sitting in a puddle of water. There was no driver's seat to sit on. Someone had broken into his car and swiped both front bucket seats. At least the crook left him the radio and clock imbedded in the dashboard. What kind of demented person would pull such a stunt, on Thanksgiving no less?

A glimpse back at the doctor's office made Slayter's stomach jump. Dr. Sinn was staring at him through the lab window. Clearly, the doctor's spy had been directed to steal his front car seats as part of his retribution. Merely poisoning him wasn't good enough.

Slayter rarely lost his temper. He couldn't remember ever exchanging blows with another person. Someone would always jump in and break up the fight before a punch was thrown. Or an expression of fear would suddenly appear on his opponent's face, and they would back off. Every so often while horsing around, he would give an adversary a head noogie or underwear-wedgie, also called a Melvin.

His first inclination, after speeding away from the doctor's office, was to go back and mop the floor with Dr. Sinn until the doctor created another batch of permanent antidote.

Slayter reviewed Dr. Sinn's rules. Was he willing to gamble his life on a do or die move? He glared at the doctor. A baseball hitter stepping into the batter's box would have a better chance of hitting a blazing fastball with his eyes closed than Slayter had if he tried to force the doctor into preparing another antidote. There had to be a safer way for him to proceed. He squinted up to the heavens and made a vow: if he ever got out of this mess, he would return and give Dr. Sinn a noogie and a Melvin on general principle.

Slayter stared at the inside of his violated car. His Bug looked naked without the front bucket seats. Renegade shards formed an outline of where the driver's seat had been positioned. Dr. Sinn's spy probably removed the passenger seat just in case Slayter was handy enough to transplant it onto the driver's side. In reality, the spy didn't have to go to all that trouble. Slayter's fingers and thumbs were for aesthetics only. Someone had always been around to tend to his mechanical needs, whether he asked for help or not. Helplessness was a bitter flavor Slayter had never experienced until today, and he was quite sure it had little chance of becoming an acquired taste.

"How am I supposed to drive without a driver's seat?" Slayter kicked the rear metal back bumper. "Without a car or someone to help me, I'm sunk. Bobsville is too spread out to travel by foot from one destination to another." He glanced at the lab window again. "Here I am spouting that Dr. Sinn is Looney Tunes while standing in the street getting soaking wet and talking to myself. How crazy is that?"

He wiped all the shards he could find from inside his car onto the street. What if they messed with the ignition? Would his Bug blow up if he ignited the engine by twisting the key? What if he bypassed the ignition? He peeked under the dashboard. How many movies had he seen where a character hotwired a car? It looked easy enough. Just find two hot wires and connect them. Hot was the operative word. What would happen if he connected the wrong two hot wires? Zap city? He visualized a front-page headline in tomorrow's *Bobsville Bulletin*: *"Tom wasn't the only turkey to get roasted on Thanksgiving. The late twenty-five-year-old Slayter Jones..."*

Slayter peered down the block for a phone booth. Unlike Superman, where public telephones were always available during a crisis, the doctor's office was located in a residential area. He observed a series of telephone poles lined up and down the block. Each house had a telephone. He could knock on a neighbor's door and ask if he could use the phone. Most folks would help out someone in an emergency, even a stranger. Slayter scuffed his desert boot on the asphalt. Another bad idea. The spy would report him to Dr. Sinn via a walkie-talkie, which would take away any chance he had to get his antidote.

Slayter studied the inside of his car. Was it possible to drive without a driver's seat? He planted both knees into the hard floorboard between the chair brackets like he was praying. He placed the key into the ignition, held his breath, and twisted. The front of the car jumped forward and stalled, sending him sprawling to the floor. Slayter released an angry growl that would have made a German shepherd proud after realizing the gearshift was in first gear instead of neutral. He would have been better off saying a prayer.

"It's a stick-shift manual transmission, dumb shit. You have to depress the clutch while pressing down on the gas pedal." Slayter stared at the three floor pedals. "The good news, you didn't blow up. The bad news, you now know maneuvering a stick-shift is impossible while on your knees. Plus you can't even see over the steering wheel."

Slayter crept out of his car and flapped his arms across his chest. If he was telling this scene to his editor Paige, what would he have his protagonist do to get out of a similar situation? Unlike Slayter, his hero Hunter would have to be resourceful in finding a solution to the problem. His eyes did a frenetic search of the surroundings. Each dwelling came in various colors, shapes, and sizes. Nothing jumped out at him except a two-story house across the street next door to Dr. Sinn's office. The house was surrounded by a giant Tinkertoy-like scaffolding. Could he build a driver's seat with metal scaffolding parts? Without tools or a mechanical mind, he'd be better off with Tinkertoys.

As Slayter leaned against the front fender, he noticed fuzzy images of a tarpaulin, Coca-Cola bottles, paintbrushes, and a large metal container on the ground underneath an eave. He ran to the house, stood in a muddy flowerbed, and studied the empty paint can. What if he was spotted stealing from the house and it was reported to the police? Then again, what did he have to lose? If he got arrested, doing the time for the crime wouldn't be an issue. Slayter filched the paint can and hustled back to his car. He had never stolen anything before. Not only was he fighting for his life, he was now a criminal. His new title gave him an additional jolt of adrenaline.

The canister fit between the floor brackets. He tested his creation by putting his butt on the overturned can. His new seat was weird, wobbly, and uncomfortable, but he could see over the steering wheel. Wind-driven moisture plastered the left side of his face and shoulder through the glassless window. Splotches of blue paint now adorned his gray slacks, something that would have bothered him under normal circumstances. All that mattered was if his improvised seat was functional enough for him to drive.

He turned the ignition key after his left foot punched down the clutch pedal. Elvis' "Heartbreak Hotel" blasted from the radio speaker. Elvis wasn't the only guy who was so lonely he could die. Slayter popped the clutch and jammed down the gas pedal. The momentum sent him flying backwards off the can, causing the engine to stall once more.

Slayter removed himself from the backseat and mounted the container again. His left hand took hold of the steering wheel. His right hand turned off the radio and grabbed the gearshift knob. Left foot pushed the clutch in, right pressed the gas pedal. His little Bug crept forward without stalling. Slayter straightened his back. Mastering how to drive a stick shift on a metal paint can was a significant victory. He notched up the speed enough to shift into second gear. If he had a free hand, he would have patted himself on the back. Someday they will put a man on the moon. Until that day happens, driving without a driver's seat was an accomplishment worthy of cheers and applause for a moon landing. He slowed for a right turn, leaned his body to the right, and fell off the can. The engine shut down in the middle of the street. The cheers in his head turned to boos after learning he had to lean in the opposite direction while turning. He went through the process of restarting the engine, but his right foot jumped off the gas pedal and onto the brake when he noticed the gas gauge. The motor idled after he pushed the gearshift into neutral.

"Damn!" The gas needle was kissing the E. How could that be? He had over a quarter tank of gas when he arrived at Dr. Sinn's office earlier. Or maybe he didn't. Slayter flicked a finger against the gauge's glass several times, but the needle never moved. Gas was evaporating from his tank along with precious seconds ticking away while his brain was stuck in neutral. A momentary look into the driver's side mirror confirmed his earlier conviction. The gas cap was missing.

"Holy schnickeys! Dr. Sinn's spy vandalized my car, stole the front bucket seats, and siphoned gas from the tank." He stared at the gauge needle again. A hair below empty. "My car is running on fumes. Is there even one gas station open on Thanksgiving night?"

A pair of high-beam headlights shined in his rearview mirror. He couldn't make out who was inside the vehicle, but the driver didn't honk for Slayter to move his car from the middle of the road. Slayter would bet every cent he had in his pockets - which consisted of three dimes - the driver behind him was Dr. Sinn's spy.

A dark figure climbed out of his vehicle carrying two objects, one in each hand. Slayter switched off the engine and looked for something he could defend himself with. He tried to unscrew the gearshift knob but was unsuccessful. He picked up the only item he could use as a weapon from the floorboard.

Slayter launched out of his car. His left hand formed into a fist. His right thumb clicked open the ballpoint pen tip like a switchblade knife. He held his ground as the spy stalked him before stopping in an area flooded by a streetlight. The pen dropped from his hand.

"You!" Slayter shouted.

Chapter Six (1955 Thanksgiving Day)

Slayter charged Dr. Sinn's spy like a snorting bull at a red cape sale. His childhood friend, Doody, backpedaled until his skinny butt was pinned against his truck, conceding he was unable to compete against a stronger, more athletic Slayter. Doody aimed a flashlight beam into Slayter's face and raised a walkie-talkie to his mouth.

"Dr. Sinn!" Doody shouted. "Come in, Dr. Sinn! Are you there, Dr. Sinn? Help!"

The befuddled Doody gaped at the walkie-talkie front speaker as if it was broken, and then he banged the radio's army-green face against his thigh several times.

"Proper radio protocol is to say *over* when you are done speaking, Larry." Dr. Sinn's edgy tone transmitted through the radio's speaker. "Please don't tell me you have lost track of Mr. Jones already. *Over.*"

"Slayter caught me tailing him. He has the look of a cat that has just lost his nip. You need to tell him to back off before it's all *over* for me. *Over! Over! Over!*"

"Mr. Jones," Dr. Sinn said, "for your sake I hope you can recall the conditions we discussed? The first condition also applies to your friend Larry. Physically harming him will immediately break our agreement, and you know what that means. *Over.*"

A slow-moving Nash Rambler with a headlight out neared, prompting Slayter to remove his fingers from Doody's neck. The male driver furnished a suspicious look while motoring around their vehicles. Dr. Sinn referred to Doody as Larry, his Christian name. Doody had not been called Larry since grade school. Even Doody's parents called him Doody. It was difficult for Slayter to digest Doody's sabotage after all their years of being buddies. Why would Doody turn against him to become Dr. Sinn's spy?

Slayter snarled at Doody, snatched the walkie-talkie radio from his former friend's hand, and pressed the only protruding button he could find.

"Slayter here, Dr. Sinn. Clearly, your doctoring my Thanksgiving food with poison was just the first installment of my sentence. In the limited time you've given me, how can I locate the poison's antidote after Doody stole my driver's seat and siphoned gas from my tank?" He paused to catch his breath. "Give me a break, doc. I can't do this without help. Please tell me who has the antidote? *Over*."

"That, Mr. Jones, is the whole point. You are on your own for good reason. Plus, if I were to give you the information you just requested, I would be breaking the bond established with my fellow mission members. *Over*."

"Will you at least tell me how many more of your little surprises I should expect? *Over*."

"Then they wouldn't be a surprise," Dr. Sinn offered. "I never said it would be easy. On the contrary, you have had it easy all of your life. Tick! Tick! Tick! *Over*."

Doody huffed out a mouthful of air after Slayter slammed the walkie-talkie into the spy's stomach. Slayter caught the scent of gasoline. He peeked into the green 1945 Ford pickup truck's bed hoping to see bucket seats. Instead, he found leftover wet *Bobsville Bulletin* newspapers from Doody's paper route piled next to a piece of garden hose.

"If I'd known you were sucking out gasoline from my tank," Slayter said, "I would have splurged for the high-octane grade. I hope you enjoyed every last drop, petrol breath."

"Siphoning gas is Yucko-ville, man." Doody's face bunched into a sour expression that made his freckles knit together, then he spit onto the wet street.

Slayter rolled his eyes as he often did when interacting with Doody. It was a toss-up who had the higher IQ between Doody and the marionette Howdy Doody.

"What did you do with my front seats and gas cap?" Slayter asked.

"I'm not supposed to talk to you, Slayter. Dr. Sinn's orders."

"And I'm not supposed to harm you." Slayter put a fist an inch away from Doody's chin. "You have two options. One, answer all my questions. Or two, you'll never again have to worry about having a face resembling Howdy Doody. It's your choice. One or two?"

"I threw everything over a fence into a backyard." Doody put the flashlight in his pocket.

"Which backyard?"

"I'm not sure." Doody closed one eye, glanced behind him, and pulled on a handful of red hair darkened from the sprinkle. "The fence may have been white and pointed." He spit again. "Good thing the gate was locked 'cause a vibrating bark from a big dog sounded when I jiggled the handle. That really rattled my cage. Then I beat feet out of there when a backyard light came on after I chucked the seats over the fence."

"Sinn's plan was to incapacitate my car so I couldn't get far. What else do you know?"

"After I removed the seats and drained most of your gas, I was supposed to mess with the engine. When I popped the front hood, the motor was gone." Doody's eyes enlarged. "Someone stole your engine, Slayter. Honest to Clarabelle the Clown, I didn't take it."

"The engine in a Volkswagen Beetle is in the rear, not the front. How do you think I was able start my car and drive? No wonder you flunked auto mechanics in high school."

"Damn." Doody slapped a hand against the side of his head.

"Wouldn't it have been easier and healthier just to let the air out of my tires?"

"Double damn." Doody stretched the neck of his white t-shirt underneath the multi-colored Pendleton he was wearing.

Slayter could hear ticking again. How much time had elapsed since running from Dr. Sinn's office? He pulled his left coat sleeve back and found a bare wrist. His watch was missing. He must have lost it at one of the Thanksgiving dinners. The Bug's clock would be his guide from now on. Good thing Doody didn't confiscate that too.

Doody extracted a Lucky Strike from the front pocket of his shirt. He placed the cigarette between his lips, struck a match to life, cupped it in his hand, and raised the flame to the tip. Slayter ripped the ciggie from Doody's mouth before he could light it and crumbled the tobacco. Doody's mouth opened as if he had been insulted.

"What'd you do that for," Doody grumbled. "Just 'cause *you* don't smoke…ouch!"

Doody threw the burning match onto the wet street and blew on his fingertips.

"Think about it, Doody. You just sucked out gas from my tank through a garden hose. Lighting a match to a cigarette dangling from a mouth laced with gasoline could have made you impersonate Godzilla or the fire-breathing man in a circus act."

"Holy smoke!" Doody deposited his singed thumb and forefinger into his mouth.

Slayter had protected Doody ever since kids started picking on him for looking like Howdy Doody. Although Slayter was able to keep bullies from beating on Doody, he couldn't stop the moniker from sticking. In return for Slayter's kindness, Doody – like everyone else – was eager to assist Slayter as best he could...until today.

"We've been friends for a long time, Doody. What I can't figure out is why you would help poison me and then violate my car."

"I'll tell you why," Doody snapped. "When I was collecting for my paper route last week, I sort of let it slip out to your book editor Paige that you was having Thanksgiving dinner with two other women besides her. She really got frosted. Started cussin' like a Firestone truck driver with a flat tire and no spare when I said Betsy was one of the hostesses."

"Doody, I told you about the three Thanksgiving dinners in confidence because I didn't want to hurt anyone's feelings, and I needed your help to pull that off."

"Well, it's a good thing I let the cat poke the pig out of the bag. Paige told me you kept... what was the word she used...oh yeah badger...you kept badgering her like some wild animal the whole time by making sexual induwindows until she finally gave in and let you spend the night. Or should I say nights."

"Induwindows?" Slayter repeated. "Do you mean innuendos?"

"Yeah, yeah, that too. See, you admit it. Paige told me she was afraid if she said no to you, she wouldn't get the rest of her fee." Doody reached into his Pendleton pocket again, and then thought better of it. "If that's not bad enough, Slayter, at the same time you were getting nookie from Paige, you were false romancing Betsy. Man, who would have thunk you could be such a scumbag?"

Slayter's fingertips rubbed his temples. Could it be Doody misunderstood what Paige told him? He often misconstrued words, metaphors, and meanings. Or he had bouts of color blindness when crossing wires. Then again, it was doubtful Doody could come up with the dirt Paige was slinging. Why would Paige dupe Doody and badmouth a client?

"I have no idea why, but Paige lied to you, Doody."

"Paige told me you'd deny it." Doody's chin jutted out. "I'd give anything to have a bitchin' dolly like Betsy. I've had the hots for her ever since you introduced us. I even worked up enough nerve to ask her out on a date since you guys was just friends. She told me she was jacketed to someone else. I didn't need to have my brain washed to understand that someone else was you, Slayter. You broke that poor girl's heart. She don't gush over you like other gals, but Betsy's crazy in love with you."

Slayter cranked out a sarcastic laugh. Betsy had never given him any sign of wanting anything more than a close friendship. He figured she was crushing on some other guy. His eyebrows arched up. On the other hand, if Doody was correct – always a big if – it would change everything. Betsy had won him over when she greeted him with a captivating smile after he first entered the Bobsville Public Library to find someone to do research on his novel. He had been apprehensive about admitting his true feelings for her, fearing it would ruin their relationship. Yet...

"If Betsy is in love with me, why would she put poison in my food?" Slayter asked.

"And people say *I've* got smog in my noggin. It really hurt Betsy when she learned you was just stringing her along."

"Stringing Betsy along," Slayter repeated. "Is that what Paige told you?"

"Uh, no." Doody's tongue pushed his cheek out. "I kind of let that slip out."

"What did you do after talking to Paige?" Slayter asked. "Don't bother answering, Doody, it was a rhetorical question. You went straight to Betsy and told her what Paige said. Then you lied to Betsy about me stringing her along for research, didn't you?"

"Correctomundo. I couldn't help it. She cried like Lassie never came home."

"I think you felt sorrier for yourself," Slayter said. "If you couldn't have Betsy as a girlfriend, then I shouldn't either. Correctomundo?"

"Maybe a little." Doody peered down at his worn Keds. "Maybe more than a little."

A lot of mud was clearing into a stream of clarity. Slater didn't know the reason why Paige would retaliate against him, but now he knew how it started. He couldn't blame Betsy for thinking he was a despicable cad. Even if she did have strong feelings for him, those feelings had gone in an opposite direction. Was Paige jealous of Betsy? How could that be? Why did Paige turn on him by using Doody as a conduit to spread her venom?

"Consider yourself a bass fiddle and Paige just played you," Slayter said.

"Huh." Doody's expression reminded Slayter of a pet dog with ears perked up, and his head moving from side to side, listening, but not understanding.

"In other words, Doody, Paige skillfully manipulated you."

By the looks of Doody's narrowed eyes, he was still having trouble comprehending.

"Paige told you a pile of horse pucky and used you to spread it around, Doody."

"You're just saying that to save your own keester."

"Paige knew you'd go straight to Betsy with her falsehoods as a means to alienate Betsy against me. Then you lied to Betsy to make me seem like a selfish scoundrel. You probably shared what Paige had said with my sister-in-law Rhoda to further rat me out."

"Wrong, Sherlock," Doody said. "Betsy was the one who finked on you to Rhoda."

Slayter's nostrils flared. More dominoes had fallen into place. Now he knew why three out of five people had an agenda against him; maybe six if his brother Warren was on board. Dr. Sinn was on a lifelong mission to deal with Romeo Rogues after losing his girl. Doody experienced fits of jealousy because Betsy had feelings for someone else. And Betsy believed Paige's vicious lies about him.

Were those valid reasons to poison him? He would vote no, but his vote didn't count. What was Paige's motivation to make up those lies? Why did Betsy's misinformation upset his sister-in-law Rhoda enough to join the poison group? How did Dr. Sinn get involved?

"Did Dr. Sinn give you the antidote to the poison I ingested?" Slayter asked.

"Dr. Sinn gave it to one of us, but it wasn't me," Doody said, shaking his head.

Slayter tried to read Doody's face and came up empty. On the other hand, maybe it was Slayter who wasn't playing with a full deck? Had Doody been duping him all through the years of their friendship? Was Doody duping him now?

A black sedan with a red beanie light centered on the roof pulled behind Doody's truck. A tall patrolman covered his short-cropped dark hair with a blue hat and stepped towards them with one hand on the butt of his holstered gun and the other hand on a billy club handle. Slayter recognized the officer's familiar walk without viewing the face. Eddie Rose was six-foot-two and not a pound over 180; the same as in high school. He was dubbed "Goat" after clutching a last-second pass in the end zone of their championship game, then he allowed the ball to slip out of his hands, sending the Bobsville Bobcats down to defeat. Eddie never forgave Slayter for throwing the pass too hard. Folks in Bobsville never forgave Eddie for dropping a catchable ball.

"Hey, Goat," Doody said. "Tough luck getting patrol duty on Thanksgiving night."

Slayter gritted his teeth. There were two things Eddie hated the most: Slayter Jones and being called Goat. Was it a coincidence Eddie had duty this Thanksgiving? Or did he volunteer to take someone's place, just like Dr. Sinn?

"Is there some kind of trouble here, gentlemen?" Eddy said in a stern voice.

"Everything is cool, Eddie." Slayter said. "I just stopped to ask Doody a few questions."

"It's Officer Rose to you, Mr. Jones. Stopping in the middle of the road to shoot the breeze is a traffic hazard. I want to see your driver's license."

"We don't have car phones like you, Ed…Officer Rose." Slayter showed his ID.

"Unless you want me to ticket both of you, either pull your vehicles to the side of the road, or drive away." Eddie tapped his billy club into his palm. "Surely, a popular guy like you, Mr. Jones, has somewhere important to go on a Thanksgiving night."

Was Eddie just doing his job? Or was he another Dr. Sinn spy? Slayter slow walked back to his car with his head down. Now he couldn't even count on the police to help him.

Chapter Seven (1958 Thanksgiving Eve)

Holy studied the cocktail coaster as if it contained a hidden message. His forehead was creased, probably from trying to figure something out. Elizabeth tugged hard on his suit jacket sleeve.

"Did you find what you were looking for in the coaster, Holy?"

"I was wondering what Slayter's mindset was after dealing with that policeman and walking back to his car?"

"I can only assume an answer, and it would probably be wrong," Elizabeth said. "Let me throw your question back at you. What is your opinion?"

"Aside from what happened to Slayter's parents when he was a child, here is a man who probably never experienced a bad day in his life – until that Thanksgiving three years ago. With his survival clock ticking, Slayter has no idea who has the antidote that could save him. He couldn't depend on the police. His boyhood friend betrayed him. You, his girlfriend, probably wanted nothing to do with him. His editor Paige for some reason lied about him. And he wasn't even sure if he could trust his own brother." Holy placed his glass back onto the coaster. "In football terms, a red penalty flag should have been thrown for piling on the poor guy. I know you said he was more than capable of fending for himself, but he had never been put in a life-or-death situation before. Was he about to abandon the struggle, throw in the towel, and admit defeat? Or was he ready to accept the challenge before him?"

"I can answer those last two questions by telling you what happened next," Elizabeth said.

"By all means, please continue."

Chapter Eight (1955 Thanksgiving Day)

Slayter would have bet his last dime Officer Eddie Rose was scowling at him when the patrol car coasted by. He settled onto his jerry-rigged driver's seat and followed Eddie until the cruiser's taillights disappeared. Was the whole darn town part of an alliance against him? He was probably being paranoid, but he wouldn't chance his last dime on it.

The headlights beamed a clear path ahead. Worn windshield wipers scraped against the glass in a rhythmic beat, sending beads of water scurrying to both sides. He never bothered to turn the radio back on, but lyrics to a rock 'n roll song resonated in his head: "*With his ride in gear and nothing to fear, all he needed to know is where to go.*" He had a lot to fear, including not a hint as to which person he should deal with first.

Slayter pulled over to the curb. Dr. Sinn's spy, Doody, followed suit by parking behind him. The street sign name on the corner caused Slayter to take a second look: Stufft Lane had been named for former Bobsville Mayor Phil Stufft, before the mayor became an ex-mayor after being arrested for stuffing his pockets with embezzled city funds.

7:49 on the dashboard clock. Gone forever were nineteen invaluable minutes Slayter could never get back since he left Dr. Sinn's office. His time, and maybe his life, was ticking away at supersonic speed, and he still didn't have a plan.

Slayter rocked back and forth on the canister. More often than not, folks would facilitate things for him without his even asking. Up until today, he never considered the drawbacks of living an entitled life since childhood. Being dependent on so many people had made him unprepared for the predicament he was in. With no warning, boom, he was expected to go cold turkey and change his life in three hours without assistance. Should he ignore Dr. Sinn's conditions and find someone to help him? Slayter closed his eyes and tried to concentrate. Who could he get? His list of people had been greatly shortened. If he couldn't depend on the police, his brother, sister-in-law, book editor, boyhood friend, and a young woman he considered his best friend, who could he rely on?

He stopped rocking. At this point, the only person he could depend on was himself, a frightening thought. Slayter Jones, the ultimate enablee, would now have to turn himself into a creative, clue-finding sleuth and deal-closing salesman to find the person who has the antidote and talk that individual into cooperating with him.

The rearview mirror revealed the truck's cab light was on. Doody sucked on an unlit cigarette. By his own admission, Doody eliminated himself from Slayter's antidote hunt. The medicine Slayter was seeking came in powder form. What were the odds Doody would get confused and mix the antidote in with his morning Malt-O-Meal?

Which one of the three Thanksgiving hostesses should he seek out first? He was grateful to be working with his book editor Paige Turner. She taught him many of the do and don'ts of crafting a novel. He was amazed by her ability to listen to his recorded verbal story, chapter by chapter, and then compose the words into typed pages without losing his writer's voice and content. Paige was ten years older than him with a figure that would make Hugh Hefner blink twice. She often implied their business arrangement could be more personal if he was game. Yet this whole debacle had been prompted by her lie that blatantly misrepresented him with the people he was closest to, making her a dubious choice. Was Paige resentful because he disregarded her offer?

Without question, his best friend Betsy would have been his first choice, but her once loyal and open heart had been poisoned by Doody's loose lips that spread Paige's falsehoods.

The process of elimination left Rhoda. She was the logical person to see first, even in an illogical situation. Why would his sister-in-law get involved in poisoning him? Slayter popped the clutch and headed for home where the Thanksgiving fiasco began over six hours ago. It seemed like days instead of hours. Doody followed with his truck's cab light on and the headlights off – Doody's way of traveling incognito.

"Holy guacamole!" He squinted at the dashboard gas gauge. The needle was on the wrong side of the E. "Change of plans."

He turned towards downtown. The three dimes in his pocket would get him more than a gallon of gas if any of the four gas stations in town were open on Thanksgiving night. He zoomed past Bobsville High School and the football field where he once played. Two blocks later, a right turn put him onto Bobaloo Boulevard, the main street.

Growing up in Bobsville, downtown businesses and buildings had become treasured landmarks to Slayter. To his left across the street, Richfield Gas was the station he favored most out of the four, but it was closed. Two doors down the block was Reed's Book Emporium, one of his favorite hangouts since he was a voracious reader. The front window continued to promote *Lolita*, a scandalous new novel of delusion, obsession, and lust. Doody couldn't put *Lolita* down. Before it was published and for sale, Doody's literary favorites were *Adventures of Superman* comic books and *Mad Magazine*.

The Bank of Bobsville was on the corner holding Slayter's life's savings amounting to thirty-six dollars and two cents. Next door to the B of B stood Yoo Mortuary. He went to school with Mr. and Mrs. Yoo's son, Barry. The poor kid couldn't walk down a hallway without being teased. Slayter shook his head. Was he destined to be their next customer?

Bad Day at Black Rock starring Spencer Tracy and Robert Ryan was still on the movie theater marquee. It was also a bad day starring Slayter Jones. He had taken Betsy to the popular movie. She enjoyed it so much, he promised to take her again. A lump lodged in his throat. If he survived the mess he was in, how could he ever fill the void of not having Betsy in his life?

The Union 76 Gas Station was closed. That wasn't a big surprise. Unless folks were heading out of town, why would gas stations open their pumps on Thanksgiving when most families were grazing on turkey and all the fixings in their warm and dry homes? Slayter eyed the gas gauge again. The needle looked like it had nudged lower. He shifted into fourth gear to save precious gas.

The Volkswagen chugged past Big Bertha's Bodacious Burgers. Since it was the scene of his parent's horrible demise years ago,

Slayter and his brother Warren were probably the only two Bobsville residents who didn't partake in Bodacious Burgers. For Slayter, one day his parents were there, and the next day they were gone and never coming back. He was able to adjust to their unpredictable and shocking death because he was young and had Warren to take their place. Warren doted on him even more than his mother did, as well as becoming the provider just like their father.

Slayter eased his foot off the accelerator and coasted until the motor lugged near tricycle speed. He downshifted to keep the engine from stalling. A portion of Archie's Flying B Gas Station's tall sign came into view from two blocks away. The Flying B was his best bet to be open on Thanksgiving Day. Archie almost never closed his station, even on holidays. Keeping the station open had nothing to do with accommodating loyal customers who were in desperate need of his services and everything to do with feeding his hungry cash register. Slayter offered a short prayer to the gasoline gods that Archie's need for greed was still intact.

Slayter's foot pushed hard on the gas pedal; a do or die move. The front of his car surged forward and then coughed its last cough until it ceased moving. Doody's truck barely avoided an accident by braking to a stop inches away from the Volkswagen's back end.

Slayter wiggled the gearshift into neutral. The paint can tipped from one side to another as he hurried out of his car. He gripped the steering wheel through the open window and thrust his momentum forward. Manually pushing the Bug was like moving half a normal car. Doody's truck followed a car-length behind. A white sedan motored towards Slayter from the opposite direction. He paused to wave his arms, but the driver never slowed to offer assistance. Had everyone in town been warned not to help him? He had gone from well accepted and popular to lonesome and loathsome.

A portion of Archie's Flying B Gas Station came into view. From Slayter's vantage point, he couldn't see a single vehicle or person on the property. Was it possible that Archie would pick this day of all days to be closed? If that was the case, Slayter would have to expend more time and energy propelling his car two more blocks to the Texaco station that was, in all likelihood, closed like the other stations.

He trudged through a stop sign and the intersection. It seemed odd trotting along the side of his car in the middle of the street. His legs pumped harder until The Flying B property came into full view. Breathing hard, he maneuvered his car up the sidewalk embankment and onto Archie's pavement. All four tires rolled over a black hose prompting a *ding-ding* in front of the regular gas pump. Doody's truck stopped to hug the sidewalk curb.

Outdoor lights above the station's office and garage illuminated the front. There wasn't another car in sight, and all of the gas pumps were secured by sturdy-looking metal locks.

Slayter's eyes searched the empty grounds for anything that could break the lock and free the pump to stuff thirty cents worth of gas into his thirsty Bug.

Chapter Nine (1955 Thanksgiving Day)

The only tool Slayter could find unattached at Archie's Flying B Gas Station was a long-handled rubber squeegee soaking in a bucket. The wiper was meant to clean windshields, not to break sturdy metal locks. He gazed at the empty street. What were his options? If Archie wasn't open for business, most likely the Texaco Station would also be closed.

The station's office door burst open to reveal Archie holding a teenage girl's hand. The fingers on his other hand gripped a Nehi Orange soda. He was wearing greasy overalls, a grotty red baseball cap covering curly salt-and-pepper hair, and his usual dour expression.

"Hallelujah!" Slayter dropped the squeegee back into the bucket and peered up at the dark sky. The station was open. His luck was finally beginning to change for the better...

Or maybe not. Slayter's optimism quickly diminished when he realized Archie was holding the girl's forearm, not her hand, and they were in a loud shouting dispute. The angry girl tried to pull away from his grasp with no success. She kicked Archie's shin, which caused him to howl like a banshee and hop up and down on one leg, forcing a splash of orange liquid from the bottle.

Slayter leaned into his car and hit the steering wheel horn to get the owner's attention. Normally, Archie would saunter up to a driver and ask, "What'll it be, Bub?" Slayter hit the horn again. Archie continued to ignore him. Whatever problem Archie was having with the girl, Slayter's predicament was far more critical.

As he marched towards Archie, The *Bobsville Bulletin*'s front-page headline in the newspaper stand caught his attention: *"Percy the Pig Strikes Again."* A wild pig had been assaulting Bobsville and its citizenry for weeks.

"Archie," Slayter barked. "I need gas, and I need it now."

"You'll just have to wait until I'm done with this one, Bub."

"Get your cootie hands off of me." The girl's lips curled as she tried to pry away Archie's grip with her free hand. "It's not fair. What's a soda pop to you, anyway?"

"I'll tell ya what that soda is to me, ya little thief." Archie's grasp had lowered to the girl's wrist. "I grew up during the Great Depression. Every penny counted. You youngins today don't know the value of money, even one thin Roosevelt dime. If I let everybody steal ten cents from me, I'd be out of business. It ain't just the money. It's the principle."

The girl couldn't be more than fourteen or fifteen years old. Archie was dealing with a minor who had a major mouth. Her short brunette hair was cut similar to movie star Audrey Hepburn. She had hazel-colored eyes and a cute face dotted with pimples on her cheeks. Smudges of dirt covered her white t-shirt, pedal pusher jeans, and tennis shoes. A gaggle of goose bumps migrated on both arms. Her glare shifted from Archie to Slayter.

"You just gonna stand there and let this old geezer manhandle me? I need help."

Slayter's eyes narrowed in annoyance. Her plea sounded familiar and quite pitiful when it came out of another person's mouth. The quarrel seemed so petty compared to what he was up against. Talk about being unfair. He considered confiding in Archie about the situation he had been forced into. Then again, the girl's plight made him realize he was up against another problem. If a priest listened to his confession, the man of God would probably disbelieve his story about a group of people purposely poisoning him and recommend Slayter should drink more holy water at a funny farm chapel. How could he make Archie, or anyone else, understand he was the one in dire need of immediate help?

"I've got my own problems," Slayter said to the girl as he gazed at the orange Nehi bottle in Archie's hand. "Is it true that you swiped the soda from Archie?"

She nodded and blinked several times, trying to hold back tears pooling in her eyes.

"Listen to me, Archie," Slayter said. "My gas tank is empty. No bull, I'm in a do or die situation and I'm running out of time. Would you please put aside your little differences with the young lady in order for me to buy gas?"

"She may be young, but she ain't no lady. And it don't look like you're in any kind of dire straights to me, Bub, 'cept ya got paint on your pants. You'll have to wait your turn."

"Are you really going to die?" the girl said in a softer tone. "You got gallstones or some kind of infectious disease?" She leaned away from Slayter.

Slayter had to hold back a smile. She was the first person on this Thanksgiving night to show compassion for him, even if she was fearful that he might be contagious.

"Nothing like that," Slayter said. "If you would just give him ten cents, he'll let you go."

"I don't have a dime," she admitted.

"She done stole the Nehi off my counter in the office when I had my back turned. I had to chase her down. She would've gotten away if she hadn't slipped in the mud. I'm gonna call the police and have the little thief arrested."

"Since you got your soda back, it's not technically a theft anymore," Slayter said.

The girl's eyes brightened. Her chin jutted out as if to say "nanner, nanner" to Archie.

"Ain't buying it," Archie said. "She still stole from me. Plus some of the soda spilled."

"What's your name?" Slayter asked the girl. "And why did you take his soda?"

"Nancy. I ran away from home and haven't had anything to eat or drink since last night."

"Maybe if you apologize to Archie, he will forget the whole orange soda matter, and I can buy some gas."

"No sob story is gonna change my mind," Archie said. "The only way this juvenile delinquent is gonna learn her lesson is to go to reform school."

Slayter had to remind himself that Nancy's dilemma wasn't his problem. He needed Archie much more than she did. Her shoulders slumped in defeat, as if she had given up. At least Dr. Sinn had allowed him three hours worth of hope. Right now she had none. Slayter turned to face Doody in the truck and waved his arms. Doody raised the *Lolita* novel in front of his face, reminding Slayter once again he was on his own.

Archie was punishing two people without realizing it. Slayter removed a dime from his pocket and held it out to Archie. Was he about to make the biggest mistake in his life?

"Here's your dime for the Nehi soda," Slayter announced to Archie.

Archie studied the small Liberty Head dime in Slayter's hand. His Adam's apple jutted in and out. He frowned at Nancy and released his fingers from her wrist to nab Slayter's coin.

"Okay, now we're even." Archie exposed a missing front tooth as he deposited the dime into his pocket.

Nancy rubbed her bare arms, shivering.

"Not quite," Slayter said. "Since the soda has now been paid in full, it belongs to Nancy. Please give it back to her."

"After what she did to me? No way, Bub. That's what she gets for stealing."

"Who is stealing from whom?" Slayter asked. "Do you want it spread around town you cheated a girl not even old enough to drive over a measly almost-full orange soda?"

Slayter gave Archie a steely-eyed stare conveying dead seriousness. Inside, his gut was churning to the tune of Elvis' "All Shook Up." Would Slayter even be around to spoil Archie's reputation if he resisted?

"All right, you made your point." Archie hitched his head towards Slayter's car after he handed Nancy the soda. "What's it gonna be, Bub?"

"Hold on, Archie." Slayter placed his sports coat over Nancy's shoulders. "Why did you run away from home?"

"Thanks." Nancy snuggled into the jacket that was almost long enough to be a trench coat and did a little warm-up dance. "I got in a big fight with my stepmother. She really pisses me off. She makes me do chores. Gets on my case about studying. I've got a nine o'clock curfew. She says I'm not old enough to go out on a date yet, not that anyone has ever asked. She makes my life miserable because she hates me. It's not fair. My dad always takes her side. Why did he have to marry her?"

"How much gas do you want, Bub?" Archie said, raising his voice. "I ain't got all night."

Slayter pushed his palm out at Archie. "Nancy, would you feel the same way if you knew your parents were worried sick about your disappearance and frantically looking for you because they love you?"

"Now you're razzin' my berries, mister," she said.

Mister? First time anyone ever called him mister. Slayter removed his last two dimes from his pocket and handed one to Nancy and the other to Archie. His stomach voiced its opinion in a nervous way.

"I want ten cents worth of gas. That should get me over a third of a gallon."

"You're some big spender." Archie snatched keys from the chain attached to his pants belt loop and moseyed to the gas pump. "Hey, Bub, did you know your gas cap is missing? Holy Ethyl. So is your driver's seat."

"Is this dime for the candy machine so I can get something to eat?" Nancy asked.

"That dime is meant for you to help yourself. Now call your parents and have them pick you up. I don't have time to drive you home."

"It would be better spent on candy."

"If you had a daughter and she ran away, would you want her to use this dime on candy? Or the phone?"

Nancy left the door open to the phone booth. She placed the orange soda on the shelf below the phone and lifted the receiver. Her head turned to Slayter, then she pushed the dime into the slot and dialed seven numbers with her forefinger.

"It's me," she said. "Yes, I'm all right." Tears dripped from her eyes. "I-I-I'm sorry. A nice man gave me a dime to call you." She eyed Slayter and wiped her face with a hand. "You never called me your daughter before. I'm sorry Daddy has been driving around town looking for me. Please come and pick me up at the Flying B Gas Station, Mom."

Slayter didn't wait to take back his coat. He hurried to his car. Archie returned the nozzle back to the pump after transferring a dime's worth of gasoline into the Volkswagen tank. Slayter opened the driver's side door when he noticed Doody running towards him with a serious expression on his face and waving his arms.

"Why do I get the feeling I'm about to receive the sharp end of a royal shaft?" Slayter muttered, stuffing himself back into his car and slamming the door.

Chapter Ten (Thanksgiving Day 1955)

Slayter twisted the ignition key and pumped the accelerator until the engine ignited. He craned his neck for a last look at the phone booth. Nancy still had his sports coat draped over her shoulders. She was doing the Bop with a smile on her face like she was on *American Bandstand*; most likely to keep warm and celebrate that her troubles were over, at least for the time being. He was hopeful she would never again experience a sense of being unloved, homeless, and desperate enough to steal a soda. No different from what he was feeling, with the exception of the soda.

He rubbed his sleeves after blasts of wet wind made him shiver. Had his decision to come to Nancy's aid been what was best for her? That gnawing question presented a difficult conundrum for him. What would have happened to Nancy if he had not intervened? Would she have learned her lesson without his interference? Or would this Thanksgiving Day have been the turning point to doom her life forever? Maybe Dr. Sinn had been right about the difference between enabling someone as opposed to providing assistance when necessary for a person's own good.

Slayter turned to face the windshield and found Doody standing inches away from the front bumper. Doody planted one palm on the trunk hood, while waving the other hand to catch Slayter's attention. His red eyebrows crimped together as if something of vital importance weighed heavy on his brain. Was Doody having second thoughts about sabotaging Slayter? Maybe, just maybe, Doody was ceding to Slayter's side. Slayter needed all the help he could get, even if Doody was a traitor.

Slayter rolled the window handle several times before recalling the glass was lying on the street in front of Dr. Sinn's office; a stunt Doody would pull. He slapped the steering wheel. It would be foolish for him to think Doody would change sides if there was even the slightest chance of wooing Betsy away. Slayter considered three options: shift into first gear and make Doody a hood ornament; back up and drive away; or listen to what Doody had to say. Options one and two appealed the most.

"Glad I caught ya before you took off, Slayter." Doody moved to the driver's side. "Man, you wouldn't believe how thirsty I am after sucking out all that gas. Can you lend me a dime for a soda?"

Slayter cranked out a laugh and jammed the gearshift into first gear. He was in a dreadful situation, much to Doody's actions, and the guy had the gall to request a favor from him. Just another example of how Doody's reasoning was several dimes short of a full roll.

"Sorry, man," Slayter said. "You're a minute late. Maybe you should ask Archie. After all, what's ten cents to him?"

"Good thinking, Slayter." Doody raced to the office. "Hey Archie..."

Slayter sped away from the gas station while Doody dealt with Archie. For now, he had inadvertently rid himself of Dr. Sinn's spy. Was that a good thing, or would he have to pay the consequences later? He swiped a glance at the dashboard. Hands on the clock had moved at a staggering speed. He spent seven minutes he couldn't afford or ever get back at the gas station; minutes that were unappreciated until now. Every second counted.

In the middle of the block, Goode Department Store caught Slayter's attention. On a normal night, there would be a crowd camped out on the sidewalk in front of the store window showcasing the latest television set enclosed in a cabinet. A TV in the window also provided free entertainment for folks who couldn't afford a television of their own. Tonight, however, there wasn't a single viewer watching America's favorite program, *I Love Lucy*. What would Lucy do if she found herself in Slayter's situation?

The speedometer jumped to fifty miles an hour, twice the speed limit. Slayter was several miles away from dealing with his sister-in-law and brother. It was obvious Rhoda harbored resentment against him, but he still didn't know why. How should he approach her? Mad? Humble? Or somewhere in between? If Rhoda wasn't willing to deal with him or hand over the antidote, could he rely on his brother to come to his aid?

Slayter turned onto Robertson Lane. Maybe he missed something from today's zany first Thanksgiving Dinner that could reveal the best way to connect with his new sister-in-law. Rhoda had moved into Warren's house after their wedding, joining Slayter and Stubby, Warren's five-year-old bulldog that had one brown ear, one white ear, and a brown and white stub of a tail. It only took a few days for them to learn a third person living in the house wasn't necessarily a crowd, but it was every bit of an adjustment. His mind flashed back to the 2:00 p.m. get-together...

The scent emanating from the kitchen baffled Slayter. It wasn't an unpleasant odor, nor could it be identified as an aroma that would make the whole house smell delicious. Rhoda's Uncle Zeke and Slayter held down both ends of the living room couch while an anxious Rhoda prepared her first holiday dinner.

Slayter didn't need a calendar to know it was Thanksgiving. The Detroit Lions had just finished beating the Green Bay Packers in their national television Thanksgiving football game 24 to 10. Stubby camped out by Slayter's feet. Warren was wearing his only white dress shirt and tan chinos. Uncle Zeke couldn't get over the difference between the two brothers. Warren was six-foot, three inches – a good four inches taller than Slayter – and was built like a brick retaining wall, unlike Slayter's leaner frame. Their father often joshed if Warren had Slayter's good looks he would have been a Hollywood movie star.

Warren rose from his easy chair, took five steps to the television set, dialed down the sound, switched the channel to a parade somewhere in America, and adjusted the rabbit ears antenna to alleviate most of the reception snow. He had to turn up the volume twice after Uncle Zeke complained about being unable to hear the Falstaff Beer's "Old Pro" cartoon commercials. Uncle Zeke's hearing became harder with each Falstaff consumed.

Uncle Zeke was short in stature with a stocky frame. His long nose resembled the skinny end of a ripe carrot. He could be a dead ringer of the Old Pro if he donned a black baseball cap to cover his bald head, a gray sweatshirt, and a whistle that dangled from his neck.

Slayter nibbled on the last potato chip from the bag. Warren single-handedly finished the pretzels. Uncle Zeke had emptied the popcorn bowl over twenty minutes ago. Their orchestrated fill-up-on-munchies strategy was a defensive move since Rhoda would never be confused with Betty Crocker in the kitchen. Betty Crocker was a fictitious character, and Rhoda's cooking ability was also unreal. Most newlywed husbands gain weight their first year of marriage. Warren had lost over twenty pounds, thus regaining the sculptured physique he'd had from his all-state wrestling days at Bobsville High School.

A week before Thanksgiving, Rhoda's demeanor turned frosty and then shifted into brr overdrive - bitchy, rancorous, and rambunctious. Warren said her mood swing was due to being nervous about cooking her first holiday meal. He offered to make a reservation at any restaurant open on Thanksgiving Day, with the exception of Big Bertha's Bodacious Burgers. She accepted his offer with gusto. Two days later, she changed her mind and was eager to cook in spite of Warren's attempt to talk her into going out to eat.

Before Warren could settle back into his chair, Rhoda announced it was time for them to take their places at the dining room table. Warren looked at Slayter as if they were the next gladiators to enter an arena with starving lions. Uncle Zeke continued to eyeball the TV, making his arm gyrate in the air the same way a young parader handled her baton.

Slayter placed a hand on Uncle Zeke's shoulder and pointed towards the dining room as Warren switched off the television set.

"Ready or not, Uncle Zeke, it's time to march to the table," Slayter said.

Slayter, with Stubby stationed by his shoes, sat across from Uncle Zeke. Warren and Rhoda occupied head of the table seats. Everyone had an empty fine china plate except for Slayter. Brussels sprouts honored his plate; his favorite vegetable. He smiled his pleasure to Rhoda. The only person he knew that liked Brussels sprouts was his librarian friend Betsy, the hostess of his third Thanksgiving dinner.

Rhoda literally let her brown hair down for the occasion. She further gussied up by wearing makeup and a bulge-concealing housedress. Her eyes returned to Slayter's plate after gesturing to the dishes of food centered in the middle of the table. The green salad, potatoes, and yams looked harmless enough. He wasn't as confident about the stuffing and, unless he was hallucinating, something may have moved in the cooked carrot bowl.

Slayter placed a Brussels sprout between his thumb and forefinger, looked down at Stubby, and motioned a treat would soon be coming the pet's way. The bulldog's little brown and white stub of a tail went into overdrive.

"Don't you dare feed Stubby with food from this table." Rhoda's face turned the shade of the cranberry sauce. "Is that how you thank me for preparing your favorite vegetable?"

Slayter's head jerked back. Rhoda never complained when he fed Stubby with food from his dinner plate, a habit he and Warren developed as a favor to each other. There was less leftover food for the next day's meal. He didn't have to take as many antacids after he ate, and Stubby actually liked Rhoda's cooking, although it gave him horrendous gas that often made everyone clear the room.

"It's Thanksgiving for Stubby, too," Slayter said. "He was part of this family before..."

Warren cleared his throat. His eyes bulged as his head jerked north and south.

"Sorry, buddy." Slayter gave Stubby a loving head scratch. "No grits today."

Slayter placed the Brussels sprout back onto his plate and poked it with a fork. It was tender and smelled like a Brussels sprout. He had planned to wait until Warren or Uncle Zeke sampled their food and let their expressions be his guide. What the heck, someone had to take one for the team and be the guinea pig. He stuffed the sprout into his mouth, chomped down with caution, progressed to a chew, and swallowed. It had a different zesty tang he couldn't define, but it was surprisingly edible. He speared another sprout.

Warren sneered at the steaming pale turkey Rhoda had set on the platter in front of him. He lifted a long carving knife in his right hand and a two-prong fork in the other hand. He stabbed the turkey with the fork, creating a squish noise loud enough to make Uncle Zeke wince. Slayter gored another Brussels sprout. Stubby slobbered on his desert boot.

Rhoda's eyes were still zoned in on Slayter's plate. Warren sent the sharp knife down the turkey's side. What was supposed to be a carved slice of white meat ended up as several small, serrated chunks of shredded meat. Warren examined the blade of the knife, then the wounded bird, before scowling at his wife. Slayter had an urge to paste the jagged pieces back onto Tom, like putting a jigsaw puzzle together. Uncle Zeke plunged a serving spoon deep into the dressing and came away with a glop that wouldn't detach from the spoon.

"Good gravy, Rhoda." Uncle Zeke kept shaking the spoon over his plate, but nothing would fall off. "Did you mix Elmer's Glue into this stuff?" He held the serving spoon higher for leverage, then sent it downward with an emphatic swing. Most of the dressing mass dislodged from the spoon and landed on the wallpaper behind Rhoda with a thud.

"Oops." Uncle Zeke frowned at the spoon.

Stubby scrambled to the wall. He gobbled down the mass that fell onto the floor, then licked his way up the dribble clinging on the wall. His tail gyrated like a windshield wiper at rapid speed. By Slayter's count, Stubby gave Rhoda's stuffing a ten-wag rating.

Rhoda's mouth dropped open. Uncle Zeke jammed the spoon back into the dressing bowl and looked up at the ceiling. Warren stopped shredding. Stubby farted.

The telephone rang. Slayter jumped up from his chair and hurried into the kitchen. The timing of the call couldn't have been more perfect. Slayter knew who was on the line before he lifted the receiver to his ear after the third ring.

"This is Doody, Slayter. You told me to call you, but I forget why. Do you want to remind me? Or should I call back?"

"Hey, Doody, Happy Thanksgiving. You want me to do what? Now? I'm having dinner with my family. Can't you wait until...okay. Where can I find you? I'll see you in a bit."

Slayter's stomach rumbled like an overloaded washing machine by the time he returned to the dining room and explained that Doody had some kind of car trouble. Rhoda had an odd smirk on her face. He apologized for leaving, grabbed his blue sports coat, and departed from the house to join his next Thanksgiving hostess: editor Paige Turner.

The left front tire hit a pothole, jolting Slayter back to real time. What had he learned from the flashback? Rhoda poisoned his Brussels sprouts. She cared more for Stubby's welfare than his since she stopped him from feeding the dog. Someone persuaded Rhoda to prepare Thanksgiving dinner instead of going out to a restaurant? Rhoda's smirk may have meant she knew Doody would call. Why did Rhoda harbor hard feelings against him? And he was still in the dark as to why Paige would lie to Doody...

POP! THUMP! THUMP! THUMP...

Slayter's body teetered on the paint can as he struggled with the steering wheel. The Bug swerved out of control on the wet pavement. He pounded the brake pedal. His car went into a spin and headed for a giant oak tree on the roadside. There was no front engine to protect him from getting smashed in a head-on crash. Was a tire blowout part of Dr. Sinn's plan in case the poison didn't do its job? Or was it just a bad last day at Bobsville starring Slayter Jones?

Chapter Eleven (1958 Thanksgiving Eve)

Seconds after Elizabeth narrated how Slayter lost control of his car from a blown tire three Thanksgivings ago, Holy choked out uncontrollable coughs when his drink went down the wrong pipe. Streams of caramel-colored liquor spewed out onto the table when he banged his glass down. Tears streaked his flushed cheeks as he gasped for air.

The cocktail lounge softened to a low hum. Could everyone hear how loud the beats in her heart were drumming? She patted Holy's back, unsure of what else she could do to comfort him. Every eye in the room seemed to be fixed on them – similar to when Sally strolled into the lounge with a date and confronted Elizabeth about her past. Elizabeth lifted Holy's arm and continued with the back patting. She wouldn't be surprised if Sally rushed back into the lounge and proclaimed, "I warned that poor man about Betsy. I told him straight out to be careful - very, very careful. That girl is every man's nightmare. She should be incarcerated in solitary confinement on Alcatraz Island for the rest of her life."

Holy panted out breaths through his mouth until he could breathe through his nose. He cleared his throat, sniffed, and wiped his wet cheeks with a monogrammed handkerchief. He stuffed the handkerchief back into his suit's breast pocket before Elizabeth could see the last letter of his initials. His fingers encircled the glass to take a sip, then pushed the drink away.

"Sorry about that," Holy said in a scratching voice. "I was so absorbed in your story, it literally caught me off guard the way you ended it. At least I found out Slayter wasn't a quitter."

"When put to the test, Slayter was quite the opposite, in fact. He once told me about the time he had a high school buddy take his SAT test so he could play in a golf tournament. His buddy got drunk the night before the test and scored poorly. Slayter managed to retake the test and, of course, scored very high." Elizabeth flashed a grin. "There's more. During the tournament, the wood shaft on one of Slayter's clubs snapped in half – I don't remember the name of the club, but he said it was an important one – and he still won the tournament. Slayter could adjust, he just didn't have a lot of experience doing it."

"I thought for sure the demise of Slayter would have come from the person who actually wanted him dead, not from a car accident," Holy said. "That must have come as quite a shock to each person involved, especially you, Elizabeth. I hope you realize the tire blowout was probably neglect on Slayter's part. Or it could have been an act of God caused by the rainy conditions." He cleared his throat again. "What I'm saying is the accident wasn't your fault. You shouldn't blame yourself. You were only trying to wean him off being dependent on others for his own welfare."

"Just so you know, Holy, I didn't believe Doody when he came to me and said Slayter was having an affair with Paige. Nor did I accept the story that Slayter was only paying attention to me so I would do all the research for his novel. It just didn't make sense. Doody had to be wrong, as he often was, because Slayter and I were inseparable. We were best friends who really cared about each other." Elizabeth looked away to gather herself. "I loved him with all my heart, and I was convinced he was in love with *me* too – even if he didn't realize it or wouldn't admit to it. I was certain Slayter Jones was the man I was going to marry and be with for the rest of my life."

"If you didn't believe what Doody was saying, why did you take part in the mission?"

"Holy, have you ever been told something that you knew wasn't true, but there's a seed of doubt that sticks in your craw? To ease my mind, I confronted Paige. She had always been standoffish with me. At the time, I never knew why – maybe in her mind book editors were a higher literary rank than librarians. Regrettably, Paige validated everything Doody had said about Slayter often spending the night with her. That meant he had lied about their relationship. My heart felt like it was being squeezed by a giant hand."

"I can only imagine how crushed you were," Holy said. "What did you do after that?"

Boisterous laughter erupted before Elizabeth could answer Holy's question. Both of their heads rubbernecked at the same time to the far end of the room. Three couples were enjoying their spirits. Elizabeth waited until the group settled down to continue.

"I went to see Slayter's sister-in-law Rhoda. She dropped another bombshell on me by disclosing Slayter had been making sexual advances to her ever since she moved into Warren's house after they were married. My initial reaction was the same as before. I wasn't buying what Rhoda was saying. When Slayter and I were alone, he was always a perfect gentleman. We often hugged, but only kissed once at a party when friends goaded us into it. Everything changed when Rhoda broke down sobbing and said if Warren ever found out what Slayter was doing, it would kill him. Or Warren would kill Slayter. I went off the deep end and lost all objectivity by allowing my emotions to take over."

"Did you see the movie *The Three Faces of Eve*? It came out earlier this year and was about a psychiatrist who discovered a woman patient had three distinct personalities." Holy waited until Elizabeth nodded. "Do you think it's possible Slayter had multiple personalities? That he had no idea what his other personality was doing?"

"Oh, gosh no, Holy." Elizabeth placed a hand on her chest. "I believed in Slayter. When the accusations kept piling up against him, each one getting worse, it became apparent that he expected every woman, except for me, to give in to him. I lost my head and agreed to meet with Dr. Sinn and the others to teach Slayter a lesson."

"Elizabeth, why didn't you just go to Slayter and say you had the goods on him?"

"My first inclination was to confront Slayter. But how would I know for sure he was innocent of all the dastardly things they said about him if he denied them? After all, he lied to me about Paige. I'd be back at square one. Since we were together, or spoke to each other every day, I decided to see if I could detect something in his behavior that would show me if he was the Slayter I knew and loved or the Slayter they described."

"That sounds like a sensible approach," Holy said. "What did you determine?"

"Slayter acted no differently." She moved each palm up and down as if weighing them. "Either he hoodwinked me from the beginning, or his accusers fudged the truth. Who was deceiving me?

Should I listen to my heart or the people charging him of outlandish acts?

"I may be overstepping my bounds here, but it sounds like you have never stopped loving Slayter?" Holy's eyes shifted to the entryway, then back to Elizabeth. "Does your fiancé know you still harbor serious feelings for Slayter?"

"I believe most women still have warm thoughts about their first love." She closed her eyes and breathed in a deep breath. "My fiancé is well aware of my feelings for Slayter."

"Frankly, I'm confused," Holy said. "I get why Doody wanted Slayter to look bad in your eyes so he would have a chance with you. But why would Rhoda say Slayter made improper advances if it wasn't true? What possible reason would Paige have to make up a story about having relations with Slayter?" He ran a hand over his mouth. "I'm just thinking out loud. Maybe Paige was just trying to make you jealous. Or perhaps, like Doody, Paige wanted to change your opinion of Slayter to make you distance yourself from him. It seems that Paige started everything, but it was Rhoda who really convinced you. But why? Perhaps she misunderstood Slayter. Or maybe she had romantic feelings for him, and he didn't respond."

"Those are two very logical guesses, Holy. As it turned out—"

"Sir, the table you reserve every year before Thanksgiving is now available." The hostess held a menu in her hand. "As always, it is my pleasure to seat you."

"Thank you." Holy removed a five-dollar bill from his money clip and handed it to the hostess. "Would you please hold my table for the time being? There may be three for dinner tonight. Hopefully you can accommodate two more?"

"Of course. Please let me know when you and your party are ready to be seated."

The hostess caught Brandi's attention and pointed to the spill on Holy's table. As Brandi wiped up the table surface with a towel, Elizabeth checked her watch. She had forgotten about her fiancé being late and Holy's promise to pay for their dinner if she could guess his last name. Holy's name challenge wasn't a priority, but why would her fiancé ask her to meet him at Mr. B's and be so late, or maybe not show up?

"You keep looking at your watch," Holy said, after Brandi maneuvered to another table. "You're probably concerned about your fiancé's absence. I hope you are not thinking about leaving before you finish your story. I have so many questions. I need to know if they lied to you about Slayter. How was Sally involved? What happened after Slayter's accident? Was there a big lawsuit? Who wanted Slayter dead? Were you and the other vigilante members, including Dr. Sinn, charged or arrested for murder? Wait. Slayter wasn't really poisoned. How would the police or anyone who wasn't involved even know what was really going on?" He rubbed his chin. "It would be cruel and inhumane of you to leave me hanging after piquing my interest even more. Would you please continue with your story?"

"After I take another stab at your last name. Is it Ghost?"

"Great guess, Elizabeth, but I'm not Holy Ghost."

"I should negotiate the rest of the story in exchange for your last name, but I won't. Hold onto your glass, Holy, because you won't believe what happened next."

Chapter Twelve (1955 Thanksgiving Day)

Slayter's heart felt like it was in his throat. The blown tire continued to thump repetitive beats as the car's whirling momentum targeted the oak tree on the side of the road. He braced for an impending crash by death-gripping the steering wheel with both hands.

The spinning tapered off after his foot abandoned the brake pedal. His eyes squeezed shut, reminding him of the first time he braved a rollercoaster ride as a child at an amusement park. The ride frightened the bejeebers out of him, but it ended with him being safe, sound, and wanting more. Tonight's terrifying ride was producing a fretful feeling about his fate ending in a different, more destructive way.

Mud pelted the windshield once his Bug hit the unpaved side of the road, triggering Slayter's eyelids to spring open. If his fingers held the steering wheel any tighter it might break off in his hands. His foot jumped back onto the brake pedal. Mud flew past him. The base of the tree grew larger. He detected a mossy scent. The driver's side scraped the oak's bark but kept moving. Before he could blink, the bumper zeroed in on a wood mailbox post and leveled it head-on. The metal box flew one way while letters airmailed in a different direction. His car swerved to a stop facing the road.

Slayter sat stunned, taking in the stillness. Both hands on the steering wheel had kept him from falling off the paint can. He puffed out a mouthful of air, thankful his body and car were still intact. The front bumper took the brunt of the blow. After pushing open the driver's side door, his desert boots sank in the mud like quicksand. He navigated through the muck to stand between headlight beams and inspect the damage. His knee could fit into the bumper's deep and now permanent indentation.

A low groan emitted from his throat. This morning he woke up in the peak of health. His car's window was intact, the bucket seats were in place, the left front tire was full of air, there were no scrapes imprinted in the driver's side paint, and the front bumper was unblemished. His little car would be scarred forever, which wouldn't mean diddly poop if he was unable to find the antidote to the poison he ingested.

He pushed back his shirtsleeve by habit. His bare wrist was a reminder he lost his watch at one of today's three dinners. The timepiece held sentimental value; Betsy gave it to him for his birthday. The watch would have helped him monitor how much time he had left before the temporary antidote expired. Once again, he heard ticking that could only have come from an anxious mind.

The deflated tire made the passenger side tilt awkwardly. Slayter gazed up and down the dark road and kicked the bumper. No traffic was coming from either direction. Warren's house was over a mile away. His brother had given him a National Automobile Club card just for this type of emergency, but the card wouldn't do him a lick of good. If he had access to a phone, by the time a tow truck driver showed up to change the tire, he might be dead. Slayter swallowed hard. He had never experienced loneliness, even when he was by himself. Yet being this alone and isolated produced a tremble that had nothing to do with the rain and cold. He was on his own with no one to help him. Torture. To make matters worse, he had never changed a flat tire before.

Slayter wiped away annoying moisture from his face with the back of his hand. Through the drizzle, he could make out lights from a few ranch style homes in between vacant acreage. If he knocked on every front door nearby, what were the odds he could persuade someone to come out on a rainy Thanksgiving night to help him change a flat tire in the mud. The $64,000 answer to that crucial question: his chances were about as good as poodle skirts and coonskin caps making a comeback. How long would it take him to run the distance to Warren's house under these conditions? Too long. What if Dr. Sinn's temporary antidote lost its potency in less time than the doctor predicted? Slayter would be caught in no-man's land with no chance of confronting Rhoda and getting the antidote. His best bet would be to figure out how to change a tire; a daunting thought.

Slayter popped open the front trunk and found an upright spare tire. Behind the spare he discovered a two-foot metal bar with a spring coiled near the round bottom, a lever that looked similar to a crowbar, and a three-inch hollow metal tube whose function escaped him. One end of the tube was open; the other end could function as a cookie cutter. He couldn't find assembly instructions on how to use a carjack after emptying the trunk. Adding insult to his ineptness, Doody knew how to change a tire in no time flat.

"This is all Doody's fault." Slayter looked at the carjack parts and ran a hand through his damp hair. "I wouldn't be in this situation if it wasn't for Doody..." He peered down at his muddy pants and shoes. "Jeez, I sound like teenager Nancy at the gas station. If I hadn't suggested to Doody to mooch a soda from Archie, he would have told me how to change a tire. Or even better, maybe Doody would have felt sorry for me and done the job himself." Slayter collected all the carjack pieces. "I have no one to blame but myself. It is my flat tire and my responsibility to change it."

After several missteps, Slayter managed to jack up the passenger side, but removing the tire from the rim posed a major problem. The metal lug nuts that kept the tire attached wouldn't budge when he twisted them by hand. Several minutes later, he fit the cookie cutter end of the mysterious metal cylinder over one of the lug nuts. With the aid of the lever, plus a little muscle, he removed the tire. Three minutes later, he could add changing a tire to his job resume - if he had one.

Slayter stuffed the flat tire and the jack parts back into the trunk. He was spending his allotted budget of time at an alarming rate, yet he hadn't given one thought to what he would say to his sister-in-law Rhoda. Before he could slam the hood shut, an eerie grunt sound to his right gave him a start. Something or somebody was stirring, but the darkness hid who or what was out there. He reached behind the flat tire and fumbled for the lever. The noise grew louder and closer to him by the second. He turned around without a weapon. The object moved towards Slayter until the headlights picked up its image.

"Holy ham hocks!" Slayter flashed on the newspaper headline at Archie's gas station, "*Percy the Pig Strikes Again.*" He jumped up and hit his head underneath the hood. A hand went to the bump on his noggin after he landed back into the mud. He banged the hood down to produce a loud noise that might make Percy the Pig run away, but the critter kept moving towards him. Slayter turned around and pinned his back into the front of his car.

Percy snorted out a thunderous oink that most likely meant "Charge," which is exactly what the wild animal did. Slayter hopped up onto his car's hood just as Percy made a flying leap. The pig's large mouth clamped onto the heel section of Slayter's left desert boot sole. Slayter shook his leg trying to rid the powerful mouth from his shoe. Angry, muffled snorts were released through Percy's snout. Percy acted like a greedy pig about not letting go of Slayter's heel. Slayter was being tugged down as Percy kept pulling. His hands gripped the sides of the hood to avoid sliding off the car and into the mud where he would have no chance at all.

A pair of headlights appeared from the roadway. Slayter couldn't risk using an arm to draw the driver's attention. Most likely the car would speed past him without ever knowing the predicament he was in. He screamed for help, knowing full well the driver would never hear him or realize Percy was about to overwhelm another victim.

The headlights made a quick turn from the street to shine in Slayter's eyes as if the driver heard him. The vehicle skidded to a stop on the roadside, spewing mud from both sides. The driver gunned the engine, but it didn't deter Percy's grip on Slayter's shoe. Instead, Percy shook his head from side to side, trying to dislodge the desert boot and Slayter's foot. Slayter's cries for help couldn't compete with Percy's ferocious grunts and the vehicle's loud motor. The driver tried a different tactic by blasting the horn, but it didn't dissuade the pig to run away. Percy was winning the battle, pulling Slayter further towards the mud. The honking stopped. The driver stepped away from the vehicle. He lit what he was holding with a match and chucked it near the pig. A patch of earth exploded, shooting mud into the air. Percy made a final jerk on Slayter's shoe before fleeing.

Slayter slid down the hood on wobbly legs. He was exhausted and breathless. His pants were wet, hopefully from the rain. He lifted his left leg to examine his desert boot, only to find a soggy, mud-encased navy blue dress sock. Percy didn't go away empty-mouthed.

The driver lit a cigarette and plodded through the mud until the headlights identified Doody. He raised the walkie-talkie to his mouth, forgetting about the cigarette. The burning tip charred the radio speaker. Doody spit his cigarette out into the mud and brushed the ashes from the speaker with his fingertips.

"Dr. Sinn," Doody voiced into the speaker. "You'll be happy to hear that I found Slayter on the side of the road. I kind of saved his bacon." Doody thought about what he had said and chuckled. "Don't worry. I won't let Slayter out of my sight from now on. *Over*."

"How difficult is it to follow a little Volkswagen, Larry?" Dr. Sinn paused and breathed heavily into the radio. "Perhaps I would get better results if you gave Mr. Jones the walkie-talkie so he could report his accomplishments and setbacks. Remind Mr. Jones that a good portion of his first hour has expired. *Over*."

Doody lowered the radio and turned to Slayter. "Dr. Sinn says your first hour has–"

"I got the message, Doody," Slayter said. "Man, was I glad to see you. What did you throw at Percy?"

"Do you remember when you, me, and Betsy went to San Francisco before the Fourth of July? While you and Betsy went off sightseeing, I bought me a handful of M-80 cherry bombs and some firecrackers. Them M-80's are potent little suckers, aren't they? I threw my last one at the pig."

"If you had thrown the cherry bomb a bit closer to Percy the Pig, maybe you would have collected the two-hundred-and-fifty-dollar reward being offered for his capture."

"Damn." Doody banged the side of his head with the radio. "I forgot about the reward."

"Reward or no reward, I have to give you credit. That was fast thinking. By the way, how did you know I would confront Rhoda first?"

"I would have flipped a coin, but I didn't have one. So I used a different scientific method when I'm not sure what I should do." Doody removed another cigarette from his pocket, tapped it on the radio, and lit the tip until it flamed red. "Works almost every time."

"I can use all the help I can get. What is your method?"

"Eeny, meeny, miny, moe, which way did Slayter go. The last word ended up on Rhoda."

Slayter fell back against the car with his mouth open. If Doody's scientific counting rhyme method had been one word longer or shorter, Percy would have taken away much more than Slayter's shoe.

"You wouldn't believe the rough night I've had," Doody said. "Archie has to be the cheapest S.O.B. in town. That man almost tore my head off when I asked him to loan me a dime for a soda. Plus the girl in the phone booth done laughed herself silly. Then Dr. Sinn got really teed off at me when I told him I didn't know where you were. You know better than anyone he's not the kind of guy you want mad at ya. I almost had a heifer when I couldn't find your car on the road. Then I see some dummy with his headlights on, parked in the mud on a rainy night. Lo and behold it was you, Slayter. Thought to myself, how lucky could a guy get. As it turned out, you was even luckier 'cause I saw you." Doody stiffened his back to stand up straight. "Best hope that your luck holds out."

"What do you mean?" Slayter asked.

"There's a good chance you ain't gonna be able to get your car out of the mud."

"Whoa." Slayter rushed to the driver's side door. "I never thought about that."

"Who's the birdbrain now?" Doody spouted.

Chapter Thirteen (1955 Thanksgiving Day)

The tachometer needle neared redline while the back tires continued to spin in the mud. It was like running in place, expending a lot of energy, but going nowhere. Slayter stopped torturing the engine to try a different tactic. He rocked the car back and forth by shifting from first gear to reverse and back to first, alas, with the same result. He brought the motor to an idle. All he had accomplished was more gas and time wasted.

Doody leaned against the oak tree bark, shook his head, and grinned like a raccoon that just discovered a full container of fresh garbage. What did Doody know that Slayter didn't? It was becoming more and more apparent that Doody was a heck of a lot smarter about certain things than Slayter was; a difficult but true premise to accept.

"Are you having a good time at my expense?" Slayter opened his door and studied the muck his tires were mired in.

"Aha! The foot is now on the other shoe. What do you think folks always do to me?"

"Score a point for Doody…I think," Slayter said. "How do I get out of here?"

"It's about time you asked me that question. You need fraction when you're stuck in the mud. Best way of doin' that is to get a board and place it under your back tires."

Slayter rubbed the back of his neck. Doody meant traction, but considering the circumstances, Slayter wasn't about to correct him.

"A board makes sense, Doody. The only problem is, where do I find a…"

Slayter spotted the mailbox post and thought the block of wood might be long enough to span the length of both back tires. With a shoe on one foot and a sock on the other he stepped into the mud and motioned for Doody to help him carry one end of the post.

"Dr. Sinn don't want me helping you, remember?" Doody's finger tapped the radio.

"How would Dr. Sinn ever know if you don't tell him?"

"That ain't the only reason. My Keds are already a mess. I don't want to get muddier."

Slayter didn't doubt he could convince Doody to help him. It was more of a question of how long would it take for Doody to cave in? At least he now had a way of solving his traction problem. Slayter heaved the post onto his shoulder and swayed back and forth for balance. He carried the post to the back of his car and plopped it down in the mud. On his knees, he dug a shallow trench next to the tires and placed the post in it.

Slayter struggled to get to his feet without falling. Mud and rain made his clothes feel heavier. He climbed back onto the paint can, pushed the gearshift into first, popped the clutch, and gunned the engine. It resulted in the same spinning tires as before. Shit. He proceeded to shift back and forth between reverse and first. Smoke from the tailpipe or the tires fogged the back window before the tires caught a fraction of traction on the wood and made his little car spurt forward. Sheets of wet earth spewed layers of mud onto Doody, making him look like a new B horror movie creature – Mudman. If only Dr. Sinn could see his spy now.

The Bug squirmed its way onto the street's pavement. Steering was difficult with all four tires caked with mud. Thanks to a wild pig named Percy, working the clutch pedal in and out with his mud layered sock was awkward. His undamaged right shoe inched the accelerator closer to the floor, causing Slayter to tilt back on his paint can seat. From the rearview mirror, Doody's truck kept gaining on him at a fast clip until it looked as if his Volkswagen was towing the truck's tailgating front bumper. Doody wasn't taking any chances of losing sight of the Bug for a second time.

Slayter pushed his engine to reckless speed. He was determined to make up for as much lost time as he could by racing to Warren's house to deal with his sister-in-law Rhoda and, if need be, his brother. Dark objects whizzed by on both sides. The faster he drove, the more his car sounded like a motorboat. On a map, Bobsville was shaped like a triangle. Dr. Sinn's office was located at one point, while Warren's house was positioned at another. Soon, he would be leaving the city's rural area and entering several different housing tracts where the streets had sidewalks and streetlights.

Slayter sped past a darkened Bobsville Municipal Park, a place where he had spent countless childhood hours playing Whiffle ball, pickup football, and all sorts of tag games including Capture the Flag. He received his first kiss in the sand under the big slide from a pigtailed blonde girl named Molly. The park still housed an old World War II green army tank that Slayter and playmates amused themselves on. He never got a chance to enlist in the real Army as an adult after taking a required military physical when he turned eighteen years old as a prerequisite for draft classification. Much to Slayter's surprise, he was classified 4-F (unqualified for military service) when an Army doctor discovered he had flat feet. He was even more amazed Doody had been classified 1-A after passing the physical and mental portions of the exam. Doody got drafted and spent four years on active duty as a food service specialist; a cook in civilian talk. When Doody wasn't delivering The *Bobsville Bulletin*, his other job was manning the grill at Big Bertha's Bodacious Burgers.

Slayter pulled up at the curb in front of Warren's house, his usual parking spot. Doody drove by with the walkie-talkie pasted to his ear and parked in front of Slayter. The porch light was on, along with many indoor lights; a good sign they were expecting him. Slayter's head dropped when he noticed Warren's pale green Oldsmobile wasn't in the driveway. Ever since Rhoda had moved in with them, his brother's one-car garage was filled with the rest of her belongings that didn't fit in the house. Warren was probably driving Uncle Zeke back to his home in a neighboring town. The porch light was meant for Warren, not Slayter.

Before Slayter opened his car door, he noticed clumps of mud scattered on the driver's side floorboard near the pedals. His poor little car was seat-less, dented, scratched, and caked in mud. He felt similar to his car. He limped up the walkway en route to the porch. He could pass as a tramp looking for a handout with his mud coated shoe, sock, grubby slacks, soggy shirt, and wet tousled hair. For some reason, the house took on a different appearance tonight, as if he was seeing it for the first and maybe the last time. The front was bordered with three feet of brick siding, an improvement Warren - a bricklayer by trade - made after purchasing the house. A small oval lawn fronted trimmed bushes and colorful flowers. Warren must have found gardening enjoyable and never asked for help.

Once Slayter was on the porch, he stared long and hard at the front door. Normally it would be unlocked like most doors in Bobsville. The town's motto was "Not a Dime's Worth of Crime." The door creaked open when he twisted the doorknob. Should he just walk into the house as if nothing was wrong? Or would it be more prudent to ring the doorbell like someone who was no longer welcome or living there? He still didn't know what he should say to Rhoda or how she would respond to whatever he came up with.

Slayter entered the house and closed the door. Six hours ago, he hurried from the same entryway to have dinner with Paige at her apartment after Doody's phone call. The theme song from Rhoda's favorite program *Gunsmoke* sounded from the living room TV set. Warren thought she had a crush on Marshal Matt Dillon. Marshal Dillon's heart belonged to Miss Kitty, owner of the Long Branch Saloon in Dodge City. Slayter waited for an excited Stubby to come running up to him wanting a head scratch and tummy rub. Did Rhoda poison Stubby too?

He stepped into the living room. Rhoda was sitting in Warren's chair with her back to him. She was focused on her beloved *Gunsmoke* and oblivious he was in the house. She had changed into plaid cotton pajamas. All traces of her Thanksgiving makeup had been wiped away. On the small screen, Marshal Dillon settled onto a leather saddle atop his dirty white horse, Buck. The tall Marshal grabbed the reins and peered down at his gal, Miss Kitty. Dillon's sidekick, Chester, stiff-legged his way into the scene and hollered, "Mr. Dillon, Mr. Dillon," in a twangy accent. Marshal Dillon placed a hand on the butt of his holstered pistol as if he was about to shoot a bandito or Chester for disturbing him.

Slayter clenched his jaw. A grip of anxiety made him feel like a stranger sneaking into his brother's house. His timing couldn't be worse. Rhoda was already upset enough to poison him, and he was about to interrupt her favorite program.

"Why did you put poison in my Brussels sprouts, Rhoda?"

Rhoda flinched as if she had heard a ghost. The last thing Slayter wanted to do was startle her. If he could retrieve the words that blurted from his mouth and start over, he would.

"God almighty," Rhoda shrieked, placing a hand on her chest. "You almost sent me to Boot Hill Cemetery, Slayter. I didn't hear you come into the house. I thought Marshal Matt Dillon was talking to me through the television set."

Rhoda's relieved expression made a sudden turn into wide-eyed fear. Did she actually think he came back to harm her? Stubby's paws pitter-patted up to him, his stub of a tail wagging. Slayter obliged his furry buddy with a scratch and rub. At least someone was happy to see him.

"You're some watchdog." Rhoda pointed an incriminating fore-finger at Stubby who was lying on his back with his tongue hanging out and waving front paws for more tummy rubs. She aimed the same finger at Slayter. "I didn't expect you..."

"Expect me what, Rhoda?"

"It's just that you look so..."

"Alive," Slayter said. "But for how long? You never answered my first question."

Rhoda gulped for air. She turned her head towards the television set. Marshal Dillon was getting out of Dodge, leaving Miss Kitty and Chester in his dust. Slayter cleared his throat and waited for Rhoda to answer his question.

"I...ah...was going to say you look like you've been playing in a pigsty." Rhoda's eyes followed Slayter's muddy trail on the linoleum and rug, and she rose to her feet. "Warren is going to be madder than a bricklayer with no mortar if he walks in and sees this mess."

The word pigsty made Slayter shudder. Bacon would never look or taste the same to him.

"Warren is going to be even more upset when he discovers his newlywed wife poisoned his brother's Thanksgiving dinner." Slayter stiffened. What if Warren was also in on it?

"It was nothing personal, Slayter."

"What?" A glob of mud fell to the floor when Slayter waved his arms. "How could poisoning someone on purpose not be personal?"

"What I meant, Slayter, when it was brought to my attention you were doing some awful things to individuals who were only trying to help you, that really opened my eyes. I was unaware you had another side. Face it, you've been spoiled your entire life, especially by Warren. It's a wonder how you got away with your shenanigans for as long as you have. Sure, I agreed to take part in poisoning you because it was for your own good."

"Whether you believe me or not," he said, "what you heard was a bunch of lies. Was that part of the deal? You had to lie to make me look even worse to justify poisoning me?"

Rhoda's body was trembling. The storm cloud in her eyes opened up. She did a little dance like she had to pee. Stubby issued a soft cry, then he scratched himself with a hind leg. Slayter waited until she wiped her eyes on her pajama sleeve and found her voice.

"Please, Slayter, I've got to mop and vacuum before Warren comes back from driving Uncle Zeke home. Just standing here, you're making more of a mess."

Rhoda led Slayter to the entryway by his sleeve. Stubby followed. She opened the door and guided him onto the porch. He stopped the door from closing with his only shoe.

"You can clean the floors after you answer my questions, Rhoda." He tugged her outside.

Slayter was shocked when Rhoda plopped down onto the porch with her face in her hands. He knelt down to console her. She put her arms around his neck and placed her head against his chest. To his recollection, this was the first time she had ever hugged him. Was his sister-in-law using an insincere hug to cover her lies?

"I'm so sorry," she said. "I told them you made sexual advances ever since I moved in."

"Sexual advances!" Warren marched from his car to the porch. "What the hell, Slayter, you've been messin' with my wife...in my own house."

Slayter removed Rhoda's arms from his neck. Dirt was now imprinted on her pajamas. He turned to his brother. A vein protruded from Warren's thick neck. The last time he had seen that vein, a wrestling opponent at the state championship meet was sent to the hospital. Warren grabbed Slayter's shirt and raised him up with one meaty hand like he was a lump of limp pasta.

"Holy rigatoni," Slayter grunted out. "You've got this all wrong, Warren."

Chapter Fourteen (1955 Thanksgiving Day)

Slayter was no match against his brother's brawn, especially with his feet dangling a foot off the brick porch. Nor could he speak due to Warren's shirt-bunching fist pushing against his Adam's apple. Slayter had often heard that a person's life would pass before them when they are about to knock on death's door. He may not live long enough to tell folks it was probably a wives' tale created to frighten their husbands.

Suspended in the air with no ability to fight back, it dawned on Slayter why he never had to defend himself. Warren Jones was his older brother – a former champion on a wrestling mat who took no prisoners. Warren's reputation as an undefeated wrestler in high school had always been Slayter's protector. There wasn't a guy in Bobsville who would tangle with Warren. When Slayter was faced with a potential confrontation, especially in sports, his foe would back off before it started. They weren't afraid of Slayter. They feared retribution from Warren. What a switcheroo. The pulsing vein in Warren's neck told Slayter his brother was angry enough to be his assassin.

"Trying to seduce my wife is the way you thank me after all I've done for you, Slayter," Warren spit out. "Never did I think you would hurt and disrespect me this way."

Warren's snarling voice didn't reveal a hint of strain as he held Slayter off the ground. His features bunched together into a scowl that could scare away the Grim Reaper.

"Warren, stop," Rhoda ordered, pulling on Warren's pant leg cuff. "Put Slayter down right now. Honest to Marshal Matt Dillon, he didn't do anything. I, I was lying about Slayter making sexual advances."

Slayter attempted to shout out a cheer for Rhoda. It came out like an undignified squeak. His survival could very well depend on his accuser coming to grips with the truth.

"What do you mean you were lying?" Warren said, staring down at his wife. "You said my brother had been harassing you for sex. Now you're saying he didn't. Maybe it was the other way around. Were you trying to make it with him?" Warren shook his head. "I don't mind telling you, Rhoda, you're confusing the hell out of me. What's going on?"

"There has never been anything between Slayter and me," she said. "Not once has he ever looked at me the way he gazes at his friend, Betsy, from the library. Look, I'll tell you everything, but first you need to calm down and release Slayter before you hurt him."

Slayter lost the breath he had been holding. What did Rhoda mean *before* his brother hurt him? Pressure from Warren's iron grip made Slayter's bulging eyes feel like they could pop out. The pain traveling from his neck to his head was growing more intense by the second. A series of unintelligible words leaked from Slayter's mouth again.

Slayter's shoes hit the porch with a thud after Warren released his shirt, sending clots of mud onto the bricks. Slayter tried to catch his breath. His hand went to his tender throat as he hacked out a series of coughs. Stubby placed his front paws on Slayter's pant legs begging for attention. It was Slayter, not Stubby, who required some tender loving care.

"Uncle Zeke was right," Warren said, as he gently lifted his wife to her feet. "This was the weirdest Thanksgiving he had ever experienced, and that's counting the Thanksgiving when his wife roasted a large chicken and tried pass it off as a turkey. You should level with me Rhoda before I do something I may regret."

"I promise to explain everything, Warren, but you have to swear to me that you will control your temper. I've never seen you this upset." Rhoda placed both hands on Warren's forearms. "Do you swear?"

"Yeah, yeah, damn it, I swear." Warren's vow dripped with impatience.

"I poisoned Slayter's Thanksgiving Brussels sprouts."

"Huh. Are you saying you actually poisoned my brother on purpose?" Warren tried to iron the wrinkles he created in Slayter's shirt with his hand. "It's no secret you're a rotten cook, Rhoda. When you say you poisoned Slayter, you mean accidentally, right?"

"No, I definitely poisoned him on purpose," she said, raising her shoulders.

"What on earth prompted you to do such a shameful thing, especially to a nice guy like my brother? Hell, people in this town would elect him Mayor if he decided to run - he's that popular." Warren's jaw dropped. "Whoa, did you poison me and your Uncle Zeke too? Or poor little Stubby? What have you done, Rhoda?"

"Honest, Warren, Slayter was the only person or animal I poisoned. Now, honey, you gave me your sworn word that you wouldn't lose your temper. When you hear the whole story, I think you'll realize it's not nearly as bad as you think."

"Guess what, Rhoda? I lied too. I'm so hacked off I could roast a turkey by breathing on it. Presently, there is no honey in a number of choice swear words I'd like to say to you. I can't believe you whipped up a batch of poison for Slayter's Brussels sprouts."

"That's not entirely correct," she said. "I didn't make the poison I gave to Slayter."

Warren made a face like he might throw up or make someone else puke. He eyeballed Slayter, starting with his desert boot and stopped at his mussed hair.

"Slayter, you look like a kid after he played football in the mud in his best clothes. But you don't look like a man who has been poisoned. I'm hoping she botched up the poison recipe she put in the sprouts. What kind of poison did you use, Rhoda?"

"It was a special potion concocted just for Slayter."

"Damn, this is like that movie *Black Widow* we saw a few years ago. Who would ever think something like that would happen in a peaceful place like Bobsville?" Warren snatched Slayter's dirty sleeve at the elbow. "I'll drive you to the town doctor who's on emergency duty. Rhoda, you're coming with us so you can tell the sawbones what type of poison you used. Don't worry, Slayter, you're gonna be okay."

Once more, his brother was taking care of him. *Black Widow*, a suspenseful thriller, was one of 1954's best movies. Would Warren still be on Slayter's side if Rhoda resembled gorgeous actress Ginger Rogers who played the black widow part? He should probably keep that thought to himself since Warren had switched sides.

"Hold on, Warren," Slayter said in a hoarse voice. "The doctor on emergency duty today is the person who created the poison."

"A Bobsville doctor helped poison you?" Warren glared at Slayter, then Rhoda, and back to Slayter. "Both of you are nuttier than a Planter's Peanut Bar. Does this have anything to do with your secretive novel? I never understood why you've been unwilling to show me or anyone else your writing, particularly since I'm paying for the editing."

"Paige instructed me to never show my work to anyone but her before I finish the first draft." Slayter cleared his throat. "Paige wasn't pleased when I told her Betsy has been so helpful with the research and knows my story almost as well as I do."

"My plan," Warren said, "is to make a house call on this doctor on duty. If I don't get the right diagnosis, he will never be able to practice doctoring or poisoning again. I'm thinking we don't want to warn him we're coming. That might make him run off. On the way there, Rhoda, you can explain why you and this quack poisoned my brother?"

"Yes, Rhoda, you never did answer when I asked why you poisoned me."

"Does anyone have a match?" Doody asked. Mud covered most of his skin and clothes as he walked up the driveway with an unlit cigarette protruding from his lips. "My matches got wet and don't work."

"Is this your football partner in grime, Slayter?" Warren flexed his massive arms. "Doody, it wouldn't matter if we had matches. You couldn't light that soggy cigarette with a torch. Get your silly ass back into the truck; you're meddling in family business. Honestly, Slayter, I don't think Doody has enough sense to even get out of the rain."

"Sure I do," Doody said, backing away. "I've done it lots of times."

Doody backtracked to his truck. After the door slammed shut, he grabbed the walkie-talkie. What kind of verbal picture was Doody sketching for Dr. Sinn? In trying to protect his brother, Warren may have ruined any chance Slayter had of getting the antidote.

"You better fess up, Rhoda," Warren demanded. "Why did you and that doctor poison my brother? And why did you lie?"

"Slayter's friend, Betsy, came to me saying she was told by Doody that Slayter was having sex with Paige Turner—"

"I've been paying for a prostitute?" Warren shouted.

"No," Slayter said. "Paige may be a liar, but she's not a prostitute. She's been waiting for me to provide an ending that would complete the first draft of my manuscript. Why she made up that story to Doody is still a mystery I can't figure out. Paige purposely lied to Doody about our having sexual relations – knowing full well if Doody was in charge of national secrets, we would all be wearing red and calling each other comrade."

"What about Betsy, your library friend?" Warren said. "Is she also in on the poisoning?"

"Betsy has more than a major crush on Slayter," Rhoda said. "Even Ray Charles could see that, yet for some reason Slayter didn't. In addition, Doody told Betsy that Slayter was just using her so she would continue to do the research on his novel. Betsy was beside herself. Can't say that I blame her. She told me Slayter was the man she envisioned marrying."

Slayter bounced off Warren's rock-solid arm after losing his balance. He knew Betsy cared for him. And he never considered his life without Betsy in it. Different ways of saying how they felt about each other, but with a similar result. How he wished he had voiced his true feelings to her.

"Betsy and I are...make that *were* really close. Doody lied because he has romantic feelings for Betsy and wanted me to look bad."

"Wait." Warren covered his ear as if to keep all the information he was trying to retain from leaking out. "You're saying Doody, Paige, Rhoda, and Betsy all lied."

"Betsy didn't lie." Slayter said. "She's the most honest person I've ever known. She didn't believe what Doody and Paige were saying about me and came to Rhoda hoping to get a different version.

What she got was another lie that verified the other lies."

"The way I see it," Warren said, glaring at his wife, "this whole mess would have ended if Rhoda hadn't lied. What made you tell Betsy that Slayter was making moves on you?"

Rhoda bit down on her lower lip. She tried to remove a splotch of mud from her pajamas. Maybe she was stalling, hoping Marshal Dillon would save her.

"I falsely claimed Slayter was making advances because I wanted you all to myself, Warren. The only way that would happen was to have Slayter live somewhere else. We have talked about starting a family. Where are we supposed to put a baby? Sharing a room with Slayter?" She put her arm through Warren's arm. "Whether you believe me or not, I didn't lie just for me. I also lied for Slayter's benefit."

"Oh, come on, Rhoda. You don't really expect me to believe you would first soil Slayter's reputation and then poison him for his own good."

"It was the only way for you and Slayter to see he needed to be out on his own." Rhoda turned towards the front door and pointed with her hand. "The hierarchy in this house starts with Slayter, then you, Stubby, and then me. You've catered to Slayter for so long, you don't know any other way and neither does he. When Betsy, who is a really sweet girl, came to me searching for the truth that the others were saying about Slayter, I saw a way to change things around here for the better without being cast as the evil sister-in-law, even if it meant telling a blatant lie. Believe me, I was unaware Doody and Paige were also being dishonest. When they recruited me to be a member of Dr. Sinn's poison posse to teach Slayter a lesson, I was in too deep to say no. Betsy and Dr. Sinn were completely deceived because we were so convincing. I'm sorry. I wanted to be alone with my new husband, and Slayter needed to depend only on himself."

"Most of the pieces are coming together," Slayter said. "How did Dr. Sinn get involved?"

"Paige has a friend, Sally, who recommended that Paige and the group should meet with her great-uncle, Dr. Sinn, who recently moved to Bobsville. She said he was like this Lone Ranger rebel doctor who helped folks who were troubled with unethical men."

Warren's jaw dropped. "Slayter still has the poison in his system? Get in my car, Slayter. I need to confront this Dr. Sinn as soon as possible. I'll deal with you, Rhoda, after Slayter is safe and sound."

"Wait," Slayter said. "Dr. Sinn gave me a temporary antidote so I could hunt down the permanent cure. The temporary one will wear off in less than two hours, give or take a few minutes. I need to find the person who has the permanent antidote." He focused on Rhoda. "Unless…that person is you, Rhoda."

"I would hand over the antidote if I had it, Slayter." Rhoda put a hand over her heart. "Dr. Sinn didn't give it to me. Honest. But Slayter, there is something you aren't aware of."

"Get in the car, Slayter," Warren announced. "We'll find the antidote together."

"There's no time for that," Slayter peered at his bare wrist again. "If Rhoda doesn't have the antidote, then Betsy or Paige has it. I'm the only one who can talk them into giving it to me. No one else can help me. If Dr. Sinn discovers that someone has assisted me, I'll never get the antidote. That's the deal we made. What time do you have, Warren?"

"Eight twenty-six. My God, what've you gotten yourself into, Slayter? Let me help you."

"I have an hour and thirty-four minutes to find the antidote. And I have to do it alone."

"How would this Dr. Sinn cat even know if I helped you?" Warren asked.

"Doody has a walkie-talkie and is reporting my every move to Dr. Sinn."

"We'll see about that." Warren headed for the truck. "He's more of a fiend than a friend."

"Slayter, please listen to me," Rhoda said. "The antidote you're seeking won't help you."

"Stop, Warren," Slayter shouted, ignoring Rhoda. "The deal with Sinn is that no one can help me on my quest to find the antidote. Rhoda was right to want me out of the house."

"Good luck with that, little brother." Warren grabbed Slayter by the shoulders before he could leave the porch. "The first thing you need to do is take a shower and change clothes. Put another way, you stink like a—"

"Okay, I get your drift, but I can't take the time." Slayter tried to tug away from Warren.

"If you don't clean up, how do you think Betsy or Paige will respond to your antidote request?" Warren bent down and picked up the nozzle attached to a coiled garden hose. "Indoor shower or outdoor?"

"Indoor," Slayter said, inching towards the door. "But, please, Warren, don't do or say anything to Doody that might hinder my getting the antidote."

"No problem, Slayter." Warren threw the nozzle down and marched towards the truck. "Hey Doody, if anything bad happens to my little brother, you'll wish you were a marionette."

Chapter Fifteen (1958 Thanksgiving Eve)

Elizabeth's attention was abruptly taken away from sharing her story with Holy when two middle-aged couples entered the cocktail lounge. Both ladies were wearing minks – one full length and the other a stole. The furs were probably worth more than half of Elizabeth's yearly salary.

She focused on the entryway several beats longer before turning back to Holy. Mounting hunger and anguish from being deserted by her fiancé made her stomach rumble. She tried not to peek at her watch again and failed. The closest Doggie Diner from Mr. B's was only three blocks away.

"You must be starving, Elizabeth," Holy said. "My apologies. I got so wrapped up with Slayter, Rhoda, and Warren on the doorstep, I forgot that Margaret and I always ordered hors d'oeuvres with our cocktails. Please join me in some appetizers to tide us over before your fiancé arrives."

"That's very sweet of you, Holy. But I'm really not that hungry."

Holy looked deep into her eyes, then grinned.

"What," she announced.

"You wouldn't be pulling a Rhoda on me, would you?"

"I don't understand what that means."

"Look what happened after Rhoda didn't tell the truth."

"Okay, I get it now. You caught me, Holy. I lied. I'm famished. All I had for lunch was an apple. You have been so kind in so many ways, I don't want you to spend more money on me."

"I was teasing you, Elizabeth. But I was also trying to make a point here, not embarrass you. I found your polite fib to be endearing. You were thinking of me rather than yourself, unlike Rhoda who created a blatant, selfish lie for her own benefit at Slayter's expense." Holy clasped his fingers together. "Now, with your blessings, it would be my pleasure to order some appetizers. How does

Mr. B's famous meatballs, fried oysters with bacon, and Margaret's favorite, artichoke fritters, sound?"

"Scrumptious. But that's way too much food for the two of us."

"Yes, but it's a perfect amount for three. I have a feeling your fiancé will be joining us soon. In the meantime, will you please pick up where you left off with your story? I'm starving for more."

Chapter Sixteen (1955 Thanksgiving Day)

Slayter dashed to the front door entrance after a lightning quick shower and change into a clean pair of Levi's, long sleeve button-down plaid shirt, jacket, and Converse sneakers. Would he regret taking the time to look presentable instead of seeking an antidote to the poison he ingested?

Rhoda was busy swabbing away Slayter's trail of mud with a mop as he approached the entryway. His tennies skidded on the wet linoleum, but he managed to stay upright and slide to the open front door. At least he was now privy to why Rhoda lied, although he had mixed emotions about her reason. She had been willing to hurt him to get what she wanted, which made her excuse difficult for him to swallow. Yet, if he put himself in Rhoda's place for a moment, he could see why she would stoop to making up the falsehoods about him. While her actions didn't excuse the dishonesty, it illustrated how much she wanted to be Warren's number one priority, even if it meant lowering Slayter's status. Would Slayter have been this understanding if Rhoda had first approached him with her dilemma instead of lying and poisoning him? Probably not. Nor did he know for sure if Rhoda would give him the antidote if she possessed it. If Rhoda lied once, she was capable of lying again. How sure was he that she didn't have the antidote?

Doody's truck was parked under a streetlight. Warren stood in the street thrusting a forefinger into Doody's open window while his mouth flapped up and down like a machine running at top speed. The mud mask on Doody's face couldn't veil a complexion as pale as a bed sheet. Doody leaned his torso towards the passenger side and pushed the walkie-talkie in his hand towards Warren as a means for Dr. Sinn to hear angry rhetoric from Slayter's brother.

"Oh, no. Warren, stop!" Slayter ran into the street and attempted to push Warren away from Doody's truck, but it was like trying to move a freezer full of frozen beef. "More than ever, I appreciate your trying to protect me, but you're hurting me, not helping. Remember what I told you before. I have to do this alone. No one, including you, big brother, can assist me. Please, go inside and help your wife clean up the mess I created."

Before Warren could justify his actions, Slayter placed a forefinger against his lips and pointed to the walkie-talkie. Warren grunted, and then nodded. He backed away from Doody's truck. On his way to the house, he looked back over his shoulder several times before disappearing through the doorway.

Once Slayter settled into the Bug, he sped away shifting hard from gear to gear. He had no way of knowing if his speech to Warren through the walkie-talkie would satisfy Dr. Sinn enough to allow the search for the antidote to continue.

The hands on the dashboard clock pointed to 8:41; an hour and nineteen minutes to find the antidote and ingest it. He had two blocks to make a decision about which hostess he should seek out next. Selecting Rhoda first had been an easy choice. Choosing between Betsy and Paige would be more difficult. When he came to the end of the second block, he would either turn left for Paige or right for Betsy. Paige obviously had an issue with him. Her lie started the whole damn "let's teach Slayter a lesson" theme. Approaching Paige would be like passing a car on a blind curve with no knowledge of what was coming at him from the opposite direction. Yet the reason why Paige lied about him was a major missing piece to the puzzle.

The image of Betsy's dazzling smile floated before him. Emotionally, it would be difficult to confront her. Betsy had every right to hate him, even though her reasons were tainted by the fabrication of others. His only defense would be to throw himself at the mercy of her court, plead ignorance, and produce the most sincere apology he could deliver. He owed Betsy that much, plus it might be the last time he would see her again.

Slayter downshifted to make a turn. The one variable he had not considered; which lady would most likely have the antidote – Betsy or Paige? It was impossible to come up with a definitive answer. He might be better off flipping a coin, if he had one.

As Slayter approached the stop sign at the corner of the second block, he made a sharp right turn at the last second. His thoughts went back to today's Thanksgiving with Betsy's family; the last dinner. He had visited the Harpers before on several occasions, but not on a formal holiday. His experience with Betsy's family had always been enjoyable, but today he left them under dubious conditions...

Slayter winced and blew out a breath hoping to relieve building pressure in his stomach and head. The ache had become increasingly worse driving from Paige's apartment to Betsy's parents' house, which confused him since he didn't eat much of anything at either place. He was determined to gut out another meal for Betsy's sake.

The Harpers' ranch style home was located in the ritziest section of Bobsville. The Volkswagen looked out of place lined up in a circular driveway behind a Cadillac and a Lincoln. Sections of multicolored flower beds intermingled with an expanse of luscious, manicured lawn. There wasn't a leaf out of place on bushes bordering the house.

Slayter stood on the porch holding a bottle of wine that had consumed all of the paper money in his wallet. He wiped his desert boots on a doormat that said, "Welcome to the Harpers," and pushed the doorbell. It rang out with four "dom, dom, dom, doms" that grew progressively louder with each "dom," then lower with a second set of "doms."

Betsy opened the door after the last "dom." She was wearing a navy blue skirt and white angora turtleneck sweater. Her brunette hair was pulled back into a ponytail. The smile that always sent Slayter's heart into overdrive when they greeted each other was missing. So was a hug. He peeked at his watch; twenty minutes late. Was she miffed because he wasn't on time? He entered the house and handed the wine bottle to her. A massive living room to his right was stuffed with furniture more for looks than comfort.

"Betsy, we need to talk about my novel and what Paige wants to do."

"Not now, Slayter. You're late. My family has been waiting for you to arrive."

He followed her into the family room. Betsy's father and younger brother Ronny rose to their feet to shake Slayter's hand. Grandpa Harper waved his handshake to Slayter without getting up.

Grandpa wasn't a shaker, which was due mostly to arthritis, germs, and grumpyism. Betsy excused herself, saying she had a chore to do in the kitchen.

A multitude of appetizers on the coffee table in front of the couch caught Slayter's eyes and nose, including two of his favorites – stuffed mushrooms and bacon wrapped around water chestnuts. He looked away, sensing a worsening level of nausea.

"Don't be bashful about digging in, Slayter." Mr. Harper pointed to the coffee table. "Better to fill up a plate now while the getting is good before Ronny and Grandpa mount their attack on the hors d'oeuvres. By the way, the bar is open. What's your poison?"

Slayter's stomach tooted a symphony of tunes. Were the Harpers being polite about not responding to the gross noises? Did he look as bad as he felt? He eyed the back of his hand to see if his skin had turned green.

"Thank you, Mr. Harper, but I'm good for now. It was very nice of you and Mrs. Harper to include me in your family Thanksgiving."

"Happy to have you, Slayter. Between you, me, and my bourbon on rocks, if Betsy had her way, you would have a standing invitation to all of our family festivities for a lifetime...if you know what I mean."

Slayter forced a smile. Mr. Harper's comment didn't comfort his stomach, but it made Slayter feel as if he was a part of their family. To be polite, he seized a small plate from the coffee table, placed the tiniest stuffed mushroom on it, and settled in on the loveseat. If he was able to take a series of sociable nibbles, he might eventually gnaw it down.

"Are you still an assistant teaching pro at the golf course?" Mr. Harper asked.

"Yes, sir."

"Since I'm newly retired," Mr. Harper said, "I'm thinking about learning the game of golf. If I were to take lessons, what kind of discount will you give me?"

"The best kind of discount of all, Mr. Harper." Slayter wasn't sure if his smile appeared more like a grimace.

"I'm just yanking your putter there, Slayter. But I'm serious about taking lessons. Word to the wise, you can't make a living giving

away your services, or for that matter, being an assistant golf pro. You need to think about your future and a good paying career."

"That's good advice, sir," Slayter said, nodding. Mr. Harper was thinking more about his daughter's future.

"I thought you were a writer, Slayter," Grandpa said. "Betsy won't tell us nothing about the novel she's helping you with. How about a sneak preview? We won't tell her."

"Shame on you, Grandpa." Betsy re-entered the room and sat in a chair across from the loveseat. "Since I won't reveal what Slayter's book is about, as soon as my back is turned, you try to pump information from him. No wishbone for you tonight, Grandpa."

Grandpa produced a sheepish grin and shrugged his shoulders in mock shame. Slayter loved Betsy's loyalty and sense of humor, but there was nothing funny about her sitting across the room. What did he do to upset her?

Wendy, the youngest of the Harper siblings, waltzed into the family room sipping Coca-Cola through a straw. She was wearing a print dress supported by a petticoat or two. She sat on the loveseat inches away from Slayter and threw Betsy a bratty smile. He pressed his side hard against the end of the small couch. If Betsy was sitting this close to him, he wouldn't have given it a second thought.

"You're kind of a legend at Bobsville High, Slayter," Ronny said. "In fact, the last time the Bobcats played in a championship game, you were the quarterback. The way I hear it, on the last play of the game at the five-yard line, if the end you threw a pass to didn't drop the ball, the Bobcats would've been league champions for the first time. Do you ever think about how different everyone's life would be if the end had caught your pass?"

Slayter ran a hand over his mouth. An easy question to answer since the premise of his novel What If? originated from that play. Eddie, the Goat, should have caught his pass, but it wasn't entirely Eddie's fault. The play was meant to go to Rudy, the other end who ran a route to the opposite side of the end zone. To Slayter's surprise, Rudy was wide open, jumping up and down, waving both arms. Slayter, in his haste, juggled the ball. By the time he regained his grip on the laces, Rudy was covered. Slayter then scrambled around until he saw Eddie and fired the football as hard as he could. Eddie wasn't expecting a pass thrown with that much velocity. The ball slipped right through his fingers. Eddie never forgave Slayter for throwing the football too hard from such a short distance. Folks immediately blamed Eddie, not popular Slayter, as the goat of the game. When he told people he was also at fault, no one believed him. What would Eddie's life be like seven years later if Slayter had thrown a softer pass for a touchdown? They would have been co-heroes. What if Slayter had been more convincing in claiming he was to blame? They would have been co-goats. What if Slayter had thrown the pass over Eddie's head? Slayter would now be known as the Goat, not Eddie.

Paige and Betsy were privy to the premise of his novel; a story about a young man standing at life's crossroads with the ability to envision what his future ups and downs would be with each direction he took. Although Slayter's literary ladies were anxious to learn how What If? ended, he had not shared it with anyone.

"You asked a thought-provoking question, Ronny," Slayter said. "There's no use crying over spilled milk or dropped passes. They say baseball is a game of inches. Same goes for every other sport I can think of, except chess. You win some and you lose some."

The three clichés Slayter spouted would have made famous football coach Knute Rockne roll over in his grave; four clichés including rolling over in his grave. He wanted to steer the Harpers away from what his novel was about until he shared the ending with Betsy.

"So handsome and modest too," Wendy gushed. She snuggled closer to Slayter.

The family laughed, except for Betsy. Slayter ignored Wendy's flirt. His stomach was giving him its two-minute warning. He wobbled to his feet, dizzy.

"Could you please point out which way is the bathroom?" Slayter's voice oozed with urgency as he put his plate down on the coffee table hard enough to make the mushroom bounce.

"Down the hall to the left, Slayter," Mr. Harper said.

Slayter rushed from the room afraid he wouldn't make it on time. He opened and closed the bathroom door almost in one motion. It was a tossup which order of his body needed attention first, but he was about to find out in a hurry.

*****

One look into the bathroom mirror confirmed what Slayter already knew; he was one sick ex-quarterback. His face had an ashy, gray-green tint. He wasn't sure if the Harper guest bathroom would ever be the same. For that matter, he wasn't sure he would ever be the same. The expensive-looking hand towels he used to clean up were soaking wet and crumpled in the corner by the toilet. He didn't have the stomach to pick them up yet. A cool breeze made him shiver. At least he had had the foresight to open the window before Mount Slayter exploded from different angles.

"Slayter!" Betsy said, after knocking. "You've been in there a long time. Are you okay?"

"Sure, Betsy." Slayter was embarrassed he had been in the bathroom for over ten minutes. If he could, he would flush himself down the toilet. "I'll be out in a minute."

"Mother and Grandma Harper are ready to bring out the turkey and all the fixings. They have prepared enough food to feed the Salvation Army. Please hurry."

Slayter gagged. He removed his watch and placed it on the sink. He scrubbed his hands again and then threw cold water on his face hoping to produce a normal color. No such luck. He looked for an unused towel to dry his hands and face, but he had used them all.

"What a revolting development!" Slayter grunted out, quoting the Chester B. Riley character from the Life of Riley radio and television shows. He shook his hands over the sink. "How am I going to face Betsy and her family?"

Slayter moved gingerly into the family room. Every set of Harper eyes were fixed on him, including Mrs. Harper and Grandma Harper. He should apologize, say goodbye as quickly as possible, and leave before there was another eruption. Betsy would surely understand. She was the most forgiving person he had ever met.

"You poor dear," Mrs. Harper said, taking Slayter's arm and leading him into the dinning room with Betsy on his opposite side. The Harper men followed them.

"Thank you, Mrs. Harper. I think it would be better for me to leave—"

"It's your stomach, isn't it? Mothers instinctively know these things. It's okay, Slayter."

Slayter gritted his teeth. Wait until Mrs. Harper sees her guest bathroom. He sat down. Since childhood, women of all ages felt sorry for him and offered motherly support. He never resented their instincts. On the contrary, he expected it.

"I am having a bit of stomach trouble, Mrs. Harper. I think it would be best—"

"I'll get you a bicarbonate. Now take your place at the dining room table and relax."

Mrs. Harper winked at her daughter. "Come with me, Betsy. We'll be right back."

Grandpa and Ronny took their seats at the table. Mr. Harper poured wine into long-stem wine glasses. Slayter put his hand over his glass when Mr. Harper came to him.

"When I was a kid," Grandpa said, "I swiped a homemade apple pie that was cooling on a windowsill from a nearby neighbor. By the time I got home the whole pie was gone. I was sicker than a pregnant woman carrying triplets and dealing with morning sickness. I mean to tell you, my stomach hurt so bad that I was up-chucking a trail of—"

"We get your point, Grandpa," Mr. Harper interrupted.

Slayter's cheeks expanded, trying to hold back whatever was left in his stomach. Wendy carried in a bowl of mashed potatoes and placed it in the middle of the table. Grandma Harper held a large platter with a turkey browned to perfection. She set it in front of Mr. Harper for carving. Mrs. Harper handed Slayter a glass of fizzing bubbles.

"This should take care of your problem," Mrs. Harper said. "Drink up, Slayter."

Betsy arrived with a covered Corning Ware bowl and placed it next to Slayter's plate.

"Betsy made this special just for you." Mrs. Harper lifted the lid. "Brussels spouts."

Slayter ran for the bathroom.

Chapter Seventeen (1955 Thanksgiving Day)

Halfway into the intersection Slayter realized he ran through a stop sign without even slowing. His mind had been so absorbed in rehashing Thanksgiving with Betsy's family, he wasn't paying attention to his driving. He was lucky there wasn't any cross traffic, otherwise his Bug would have been squished with him in it.

The scraping of his windshield wipers was becoming more annoying with each swipe. Months ago, for his birthday, Doody had promised to replace the old wipers with new ones. Every time it rained, Slayter made a memo in his mind to pester Doody about the wipers. By the time Doody got around to fulfilling his gift promise, Slayter would have another birthday. Doody's neglect was yet another example of why Slayter was in this unnerving predicament. Instead of depending on Doody, he should have replaced the windshield wipers himself.

The truck grew larger in the rearview mirror. Doody had come to a complete stop instead of running the stop sign. Any thought Slayter had of distancing himself from the truck vanished. His gas gauge needle was creeping toward empty again. The fuel-efficient Bug always got him there and back, but the gas guzzling truck with a larger engine and gas tank got Doody there and back faster.

A feeling of nausea made Slayter place a hand on his stomach after he recalled his experience at the Harpers' house. He would rather have played hurt in a football game with a sprained ligament or a broken bone than suffer through another bout of Dr. Sinn's revenge potion. When Slayter left Paige's apartment feeling worse by the minute, he considered calling Betsy to tell her he was too ill to attend her family's Thanksgiving dinner. He simply didn't want to disappoint her. If only he'd gone with his first instinct. Yet, as it turned out, he had hurt Betsy in a much different way.

Looking back, there had been several signs he should have detected to warn him that something was amiss. Foresight is better than hindsight in most cases. Rhoda had never complained about feeding Stubby at the dinner table. Yet he blamed Rhoda's inability as a cook on his initial symptoms as he left the house. Paige had thrown enough guilt darts to prompt Slayter to eat what she prepared just for him. His stomach pain worsened twofold after leaving Paige's apartment. But the biggest eye-opening tip-off should have been Betsy's distant response after she greeted him at the door.

Slayter pushed down harder on the accelerator, angry at himself. Maybe if he had felt better, he would have caught some or all of the clues, but there was no way he could have realized Betsy's opinion of him was corrupted by lies from Paige, Doody, and Rhoda. Nor would it ever have dawned on him to be suspicious of all three of his Thanksgiving meals being purposely tainted with Dr. Sinn's Kryptonite. The ache in his heart weighed heavy on him; not from being poisoned, but for hurting Betsy without her knowing the truth. Maybe he should have had Rhoda call Betsy to pave the way for his visit. Or would Betsy think he coerced Rhoda into it? His best bet was to defend his case without help.

The speedometer needle continued to lean hard to the right. After he had entered the Harpers' home, Betsy had led him into the family room and then excused herself to do a chore in the kitchen. Betsy didn't have an impolite bone in her body. He didn't consider it rude behavior that she had left him alone to fend for himself with her family while she assisted her mother and grandmother with the cooking duties. Nor did he suspect Betsy's task in the kitchen was the last part of a well-orchestrated plot to punish him. His eyebrows shot up. What about the rest of Betsy's family? Were some or all of the Harpers in on the conspiracy to poison him? It was entirely possible, considering his best friend Betsy was a loving member of the Harper family. If Betsy could be convinced to be disloyal to him, so could the Harpers.

Mrs. Harper's nurturing care had made him feel like he was her second son. Her attractive face was an older version of Betsy, and Grandma Harper looked like an older version of Mrs. Harper. The three generations of Harper women in the kitchen could have acted as co-conspirators. After all, a tight-knit family that poisons together...

Mr. Harper had alluded that Slayter was a future son-in-law. Perhaps the assignment Betsy's dad had been given was to slip a "Mickey" into Slayter's drink? Come to think about it, Mr. Harper had never offered Slayter liquor before. Was Mr. Harper disappointed Slayter turned down his offer for a cocktail?

What about Betsy's brother, Ronny? Was his convincing hero-worshipping performance meant to lift Slayter onto a higher pedestal than he deserved? Slayter was voted to the all-league football team – so were many of his talented teammates since the Bobcats had a good win-loss record. But seven years had passed since the last game of Slayter's career. Why would today's generation of high school kids be so knowledgeable about that game?

Wendy, Betsy's younger sister, flirted with him the way high school girls are wont to do. Slayter always felt Wendy was more interested in irritating her older sister than having romantic feelings for him. Was her flirt today a camouflage for Slayter to drop his guard while the rest of the family was in the process of poisoning him?

Was grumpy old Grandpa's role to cozy up to Slayter and get him to spill the ending he had never shared with anyone, including Betsy? The reason he didn't reveal the final portion of his book to her had nothing to do with trust. On the contrary, he had been saving how his novel ended as a surprise for Betsy. In hindsight, maybe he was the one to receive the surprise.

Slayter applied more pressure on the gas pedal. He may never know how many of the Harpers had a hand in poisoning him besides Betsy. A sudden jolt of optimism pushed his negative thoughts away. His shoulders straightened as he panted out a series of excited breaths. Hope was a flavorful dangling carrot that makes a person keep turning their life's pages. What if the potency of Dr. Sinn's poison depended on all three servings? If that was the case, he may have escaped the dreaded outcome since he didn't consume the last poison installment at the Harper Thanksgiving table. He never went back to the dining room after his second go-around in the Harper guest bathroom. Instead, he excused himself and left their house to find the Bobsville town doctor who was on emergency duty. Did he need to find the antidote if he didn't eat Betsy's Brussels sprouts?

Slayter's euphoric moment ended as abruptly as it began. He gulped back a series of sober breaths. What if each dose he consumed had enough potency to kill him? Would all three doses merely finish him off faster? The only person who could answer those questions was Dr. Sinn. Slayter's heart-thumping optimism had turned into a serious case of heartburn, leaving a horrible taste in his mouth.

A siren forced Slayter's sightline to focus on the rearview mirror again. Doody's truck was still behind the Bug, traveling close to the same speed so he wouldn't lose sight of him like before. Slayter could see the red tip of Doody's cigarette in the darkened cab. The truck got smaller as it drifted back away from the Bug, and then pulled over to the side of the road like drivers are directed to do when they hear a siren. Slayter chortled. A cop just nailed Doody for speeding. How's that for cosmic justice?

The police car zoomed past Doody. The roof's red light lit up as if it was on fire. Slayter veered to the curb and waited for the cruiser to pass and chase the lawbreaker the cop was after. Or maybe there was a crisis needing police support. Slayter waited for the patrol car to blast past him, but it never did. Instead, he found Johnny Law in his rearview mirror, idling behind the Bug's back bumper with its red light still burning bright.

"Holy hot water, I'm the offender he's after. Where's a cop when you *don't* need them?"

Chapter Eighteen (1955 Thanksgiving Day)

The tall policeman stepped out of his car, adjusted his hat, and ambled to the Volkswagen with a ticket book in his hand. When he got to Slayter's broken window, he leaned over to confront the traffic offender with a smirk on his lips. Slayter closed his eyes and shook his head. Guess who was the Goat now?

"We meet again tonight, Mr. Jones." Officer Eddie Rose's lips grew into an obnoxious smile as he inspected the inside of Slayter's car with a flashlight. "I'm sure you have a good reason to be driving a motor vehicle sitting on an industrial sized can of paint."

"You bet I do, Eddie. Earlier this evening, someone shattered my driver's side window, broke into my car, swiped the front seats, and siphoned gas from the tank."

"That's Officer Rose to you, Mr. Jones," Eddie said in a tone that would make Sergeant Joe Friday from the television program *Dragnet* proud. "Did you report this crime to the police station? If not, why didn't you report it to me when we met earlier?"

"Well, I'm reporting it now. Come on, Eddie, cut the act. You know why my car was vandalized. It's no secret you've had a seven-year grudge against me. After all these years, you are now finally able to get back at me. How much is Dr. Sinn paying you? Or maybe he offered you a lifetime of free medical exams in exchange for harassing me?"

Eddie's head reared back with so much momentum his hat fell onto the wet street. He stooped, picked up the hat, and wiped the wet grit from the blue-colored material before putting it back onto his head. His features transformed from full of himself to serious, then back to seriously full of himself. He tried to hold back his laughter and failed.

"Wait 'til the boys back at the station hear this one," Eddie howled. "Kudos for being so creative – this is one for the books. At least you haven't lost your sense of humor. How much have you had to drink tonight, Mr. Jones?"

"Look, I'm onto you, Eddie," Slayter said. "It's more than a coincidence we're meeting for a second time tonight. Why don't you admit it and stop jiving me. You're part of the poison party working with Dr. Sinn."

"I don't have one iota of a clue what you're talking about, Mr. Jones. Nor do I know who or what this Dr. Sinn is." Eddie peered at the backseat. "Are you saying people are trying to poison you? Are they in your car now? Are they pink with large trunks? I'm gonna ask you one more time. Have you been drinking, Mr. Jones?"

Uh-oh. Slayter could hear himself swallow. Was Eddie being honest about not knowing Dr. Sinn or a gang of people poisoning him? If Eddie wasn't involved, Slayter had just dug himself a hole that was deep enough to reach China.

"I haven't had a drop of booze tonight," Slayter said. "Now, I have a question for you, Eddie. If you aren't a poison co-conspirator, why did you stop me?"

Eddie threw Slayter an icy cold stare. "I stopped you because you ran a stop sign. And you were speeding. I clocked you doing sixty-one miles an hour in a thirty-mile-an-hour zone. That adds up to being over twice the speed limit, just in case you are not coherent enough to do the math." He eyed the paint can again, then stepped back and inspected the scratch marks on the driver's side fender and door. "I'm pretty darn sure there's a regulation about driving on an illegal driver's seat. If there isn't, there should be. And it looks like your car has been in a recent accident."

"My car brushed against an oak tree when a front tire blew out. Check under the front hood for a flat tire. I admit to speeding and running a stop sign. Why didn't you stop Doody? He was speeding too."

"I didn't pull Doody over because you were the lead car. You were moving a few miles an hour faster than him – leader of the pack protocol. I need to see your driver's license."

Slayter closed one eye and questioned Eddie with the other. He wasn't sure if Eddie's logic about catching speeders was enforceable. Nor did he want to spend time debating it. If they were in front of a judge, maybe he could get his case dismissed because of Eddie's conflict of interest. Right here and now, Eddie was the judge. How close was Slayter to being arrested and thrown into the pokey? Any chance of obtaining the antidote to save his life would be gone. To make matters even worse, Doody was probably on the walkie-talkie telling Dr. Sinn that Slayter Jones was in a long conversation with a cop. Why did Eddie have to drop the pass with five seconds left to go?

"Look, as nutty as this sounds, Eddie, I'm in a life-and-death situation and—"

"I need to see your driver's license, Mr. Jones."

Slayter's hand came out empty after he reached into the back pocket of his jeans. He had left his wallet in his muddy slacks. This probably wasn't a good time to complain about Percy the Pig. As important as his driver's license was, his wallet contained something more valuable.

"You're probably not going to believe this, but I had to change clothes and forgot to remove my wallet," Slayter said. "However, you did see my driver's license earlier."

"That was then, this is now. I'm sure you are aware it's against the law to operate a motor vehicle without a driver's license." Eddie looked up at the dark sky. "I may need an adding machine just to total up your violations. Let's see, driving without a driver's license, failure to stop at a stop sign, speeding, driving without a proper driver's seat— "

"Didn't you hear what I said before, Eddie? I'm in a life-or-death situation."

Eddie cranked out a sarcastic laugh. "Gee, I've never heard that one before."

"It's not a lie. If I can't find the person I'm after, you can take life out of the equation."

"Okay, I'll bite," Eddie said. "What kind of dire straights are you in?"

"I can't tell you."

"This is getting juicier by the minute, Mr. Jones. You can't tell me *why* you are in a crisis situation. But you want me take your word for it. Could your reasoning be, the only person in Bobsville that never did anything for himself was named Slayter Jones? Therefore, you could never be blamed for doing something wrong. Remember, we used to joke about it in high school. If both of our hands were caught in a cookie jar, I'm the only one who would have been busted for stealing since my name wasn't Slayter Jones."

"Believe me, I'm paying for it now," Slayter said. "I wasn't trying to be a wise-ass, Eddie. If I confide in you, or any other policeman, my chances of surviving are gone. And I'm on a clock that has a little over an hour left. It's like I'm wearing a jacket filled with sticks of dynamite and my hands are tied behind my back. If I reveal my plight to anyone, the wick to the dynamite will get lit, and I can't do anything about it."

Eddie studied Slayter's jacket and shirt. "Do you realize how ludicrous you sound?"

"About as ludicrous as when I told folks I was responsible for you dropping that pass in the championship game."

Eddie's features creased in anger. The badge on his chest bulged out. He released a grunt worthy of Percy the Pig and placed a hand on the handle of the billy club dangling from his belt. Slayter tried swallowing the lump in his throat and failed. His attempt to capture Eddie's attention just turned into the match that lit the wick to his demise.

"There it is," Eddie spit out. "You had to bring up *the drop*. You didn't have to, you know? Not a day goes by that I don't think about it. Or a day when someone doesn't remind me by calling me Goat. I've often wondered what my life would be like if it never happened." His fingers formed into a fist. "You always had that magic touch on your passes whether it was in a game or practice. Rudy and I used to call you Goldilocks because your passes weren't too hard and not too soft. They were just right. In crucial situations, you always called plays for Rudy. I never was expecting the ball to come my way. Why did you throw that pass so damn hard, Slayter?"

"I knew the playbook as well as the coach, but he insisted on calling the plays – maybe to make it easier on me. Rudy was wide open, but I juggled the ball on the hike. By the time my fingers found the laces, Rudy was covered. I panicked. Then I saw you had an edge on a defender in the corner of the end zone and threw the ball with everything I had."

"You know what I think?" Eddie said. "I think you wanted to make me look like the town goat to take the heat off you. That's why you never tried very hard to defend me."

Heavy raindrops began to fall, but most of the wetness adhering to Slayter's neck came from sweat. Eddie's absurd accusations were born from years of frustration and ridicule. Whether Slayter was up for it or not, he was back to another do-or-die last play.

"When I tried to tell everyone the incomplete pass was just as much my fault, no one would listen to me," Slayter said, notching up his voice to be heard over the pelting rain. "As a matter of fact, their response was no different than your reaction when I told you I was in some serious trouble. For the record, Eddie, you also refused to believe me."

Eddie was breathing hard through his nose. He rubbed his face as raindrops dripped from the bill of his hat. The ticket book in his hand waved up and down before he smacked it hard against his thigh.

"I'm dead meat," Slayter muttered, picturing a pair of handcuffs choking his wrists.

"I know you tried, Slayter. Damn it, I've been using you as an excuse to hide my pent-up frustrations for dropping the ball. Who broke your window and stole the front seats?"

"I can't be sure since I never caught him in the act."

"In other words, you don't want to rat Doody out. I take it the paint can, mud all over the floorboard, different set of clothes, no driver's license, and Doody following you everywhere you go is part of what you're mixed up in?"

Slayter nodded his answer. He peeked at his dashboard clock and groaned.

"I get it," Eddie said. "Time is an issue, but I have to ask you this question. Besides all of your driving violations, are you in any way doing anything against the law?"

"No, I'm not. But I know at least five people who might be facing serious charges."

"Then, let me help you, Slayter. Hell, how many times have you heard that one?"

"Too many, Eddie. I appreciate the offer, but I have to do this on my own." Slayter made a snap sound with his fingers. "Actually, there is one thing you can do. Ask Doody if he knows who broke into my car since I wasn't able to give you any information. You also might mention that you are keeping an eye on him because he was speeding."

"Will do," Eddie said. "But I can't just let you drive off knowing you might be in harm's way. I'm going to follow you for awhile."

"If you tail Doody, you will be following me, too." Slayter smiled. "You best hope I survive this ordeal, Eddie. I just thought of a perfect way for you to rid yourself of the goat moniker forever."

Slayter watched Eddie scramble to Doody's truck. On a normal night he would have felt good about himself. No tickets and a sixty minute "get out of jail" reprieve card. Yet there was no joy in thinking about confronting a woman he loved who was angry enough to poison him to death. He pulled a U-turn and headed back to Warren's house.

Chapter Nineteen (1958 Thanksgiving Eve)

Elizabeth departed for the ladies' room, leaving Holy with a puzzled expression. He was trying to work out in his mind why Slayter Jones would spend invaluable time heading back to Warren's house instead of confronting the Harpers. If Holy had a hundred guesses, he still wouldn't be able to come up with the correct answer.

On her way back to the cocktail lounge, Elizabeth was intercepted by the hostess in the green dress and stiletto heels. Elizabeth held her breath, bracing herself. Was the hostess about to deliver a message saying her fiancé wasn't coming, and she would have to leave?

"Your fiancé just called, Miss Harper," the hostess said. "He gives you his apologies… again. He said his meeting in Oakland is a signature away from conclusion."

Elizabeth cocked her head to the side. Oakland? They were living in San Francisco. Both of their jobs were also in The City. What was he doing in Oakland? Who was signing what? Why hadn't he said something about this secretive meeting before?"

"Did my fiancé happen to say who he was meeting with?" Elizabeth asked.

"No, he didn't. But he was concerned that you might be thinking about leaving. He asked me to convince you to stay. He will join you as soon as possible. It must be a really important meeting." The hostess smiled wide enough to display a gap between her two front teeth. "Goodness, with all of his phone calls, if your fiancé was calling person-to-person long distance from Los Angeles, his phone bill would probably be twice as much as your dinner tab at Mr. B's. Whatever he's doing is probably worth your wait."

Elizabeth peered at the front door. Her fiancé knew she would be tempted to leave. If it hadn't been for Holy, she might be back at the apartment by now.

"Thank you for the update," Elizabeth said. "I apologize for making you the middleman in our affairs. This evening started out so strange, and it keeps getting weirder."

Brandi was preparing a doggie bag for the leftover hors d' oeuvres when Elizabeth returned to her table. Holy, ever the gentleman stood and assisted with her chair; the same procedure he would have performed for his late wife, Margaret.

"Have you ever played poker, Elizabeth?" Holy asked.

"You mean the game of poker, like in cards? No. Why?"

"It's a good thing you don't play. Your features can't hide whatever is bothering you."

"I'm sorry, Holy. My fiancé called again to say he's still delayed in a meeting somewhere in Oakland, of all places. This just isn't like him. Something is going on, but I'm not sure if it's a good thing or not. I should probably go home."

"Since you have no way of contacting your fiancé, you might want to reconsider and stay. He's coming here after his meeting, right? You will miss him if you leave."

"He knows where to find me since we live together." Her hand covered her mouth when Holy's eyebrows shot up. "No one is supposed to know that. You probably don't approve of couples living together before marriage."

"Speaking of poker faces, I guess my look of surprise gave away I'm a stuffy old fuddy-duddy. Don't worry about me, Elizabeth. It's none of my business. Your secret is safe."

"It has nothing to do with ethics," she said. "We love each other. We're engaged to be married. It seemed silly to pay two rents. Two can live cheaper than one, right?"

"That probably depends on which two are living together."

"There's another, more important, reason I haven't walked down the aisle." She rubbed the diamond. "We don't want anyone to know we are engaged or living together. Mr. Hobbs, my supervisor at the library, is retiring at the end of the year. I'm in line to get his job as long as I'm single. Unofficial societal rules frown upon married women getting job advancements over men since they might be taking the place of a male breadwinner. It's just a workplace fact of life. We will get married even if I don't get Mr. Hobbs' position."

"It's nineteen fifty-eight," Holy said. "This country's growing by leaps and bounds. The economy is humming with new jobs and innovative inventions. I have always considered myself aware of what's current and fashionable, but I guess I am out of touch. During World War II, women were essential in taking over jobs held by men. Women were vital keeping this country functioning on the home front. When the war ended, naturally the men came home and regained their former positions. I never realized the plight of a married woman who wants to remain in the workplace to retain or further her advancement. Thank you for pointing that out to me."

"There's more, Holy. Women who have a man's position often receive a lower salary."

"Doesn't seem fair, does it? I wonder what Margaret would have done if she was in your position? Of course, that was many moons ago, and things were different then." He gave her a reassuring smile. "I hope you stay, Elizabeth. I really want to meet your fiancé and tell him how fortunate he is to have you in his life."

"Thank you, Holy. That means a lot to me." She leaned towards him. "Would it be improper of me to ask if you have a photo of Margaret? I have an image of her pictured in my mind. I bet I'm not far off."

"Your request isn't improper at all." Holy removed his wallet from his suit coat's inner pocket and displayed a series of pictures at different stages of his wife's life. "To me, she was the most beautiful woman in the world."

She studied photos of a pretty brunette with long hair, a shorter mid-life hairdo, and an elder's silver shade. Elizabeth verbally agreed with his appraisal. He beamed.

"Enough about me, Elizabeth." Holy took a last look at the pictures, and then slid them back into his wallet. "You adroitly changed the subject on me. Let's get back to Slayter Jones. I'm fascinated by his story. It's like a Saturday matinee movie with cliffhanger endings that brings everyone back to the theater the following week to see what happens." He sipped his drink. "My initial instinct said Paige had the antidote and Slayter was making a mistake by seeing Betsy...oops, sorry, I mean you, first. But I changed my mind and thought you would have the cure Slayter was after. Then it dawned on me that it didn't matter who had the antidote because Slayter wasn't really poisoned."

"Yes," Elizabeth said, "but Slayter wasn't aware of that before he left Dr. Sinn's office. I don't know for sure, but I would think the clock in his head would be ticking like a time bomb on his quest to find the antidote on his own, just the way Dr. Sinn and the posse wanted him to feel."

"Slayter may have been naïve, but he was a smart guy. Deep down he must have had an inkling of suspicion he was being set up?" Holy made the ice cubes jiggle in his glass. "You have to admit, what was happening to him was so bizarre and beyond the realm of normal, there had to be a tiny bit of doubt left in his mind."

"Granted, there was nothing anyone, including myself, would consider normal or believable about what he was experiencing." Elizabeth put her palms together. "However, in my opinion, how could Slayter believe what was happening to him was staged and not real? Like the girl at Archie's gas station. Most likely, Nancy opened his eyes when he saw a lot of himself in the way she was acting. Then there was the spontaneous attack from Percy the Pig. But the clincher that may have erased all traces of uncertainty was when Slayter realized Officer Eddie Rose was not in cahoots with Dr. Sinn, and he was able to turn an enemy into an ally."

"Staged or authentic," Holy said, "it seems like the devious plan was working. Slayter accepted the responsibility of the challenge and demonstrated growth as a person."

"My view, exactly," she said, smiling. "Wasn't it impressive how Slayter won over an adversary like Eddie? Actually, it was just as notable that Eddie was able to overcome his grudge and want to help Slayter."

"You know," Holy leaned back into his chair and looked up at the ceiling, "even in negative situations, something positive often occurs. Maybe, deep down, both of them wanted to regain their friendship but didn't know how to achieve it without losing face?"

"I was thinking the same thing, Holy. Men and their jock pride. Such silliness of hard feelings over a dropped football pass."

"You aren't much of a sports fan, are you?" Holy laughed.

"Whatever gave you that idea?" she deadpanned, placing her hands on both hips. "The ironic part: Eddie Rose is now a policeman for the San Francisco Police Department."

"It's kind of amazing that you and Eddie wound end up in the same—"

"Holy," a deep voice hollered. "Son of a gun. I smell Thanksgiving in the air."

A man with slicked-back dark hair and a thin mustache hurried to Holy's table to vigorously shake his hand. He was impeccably dressed in a white sports coat, black slacks, black dress shirt showcasing gold cufflinks, and a white tie. The smoldering cigar he was holding was thicker than any hot dog Elizabeth had ever seen.

"Great to see you, my friend. Who is this lovely young lady you're chatting with, Holy?"

"Elizabeth, please meet Mr. Bobby Berger, the owner of Mr. B's. I'm chaperoning until her fiancé arrives. Bobby and I go way back to our Mission High School days."

"Welcome to Mr. B's, Elizabeth." The owner made a slight bow and then winked at her.

"You had better watch your step with this man. He stole my high school girlfriend away from me, and I've never forgiven him. I beat him out in football and baseball, but for some reason I could never win sweet Margaret's heart."

"Please allow me to set the story straight, Elizabeth. It was Bobby who tried to woo Margaret away from me."

"I have to admit he's right." Mr. B puffed out a cloud of smoke. "Back then, I had visions of Margaret being Mrs. Robert Berger instead of Mrs. Holy—"

"Not only did Margaret have great taste," Holy interrupted, pounding a thumb into his chest, "she was a very wise woman. How many times have you been divorced, Bobby?"

"Five," Bobby said. "Going on six. Don't be a stranger, Elizabeth. You pretty up the joint."

"Since high school, the only thing that has changed about Bobby is his bank account."

Elizabeth watched the restaurant owner schmooze with a couple seated in the middle of the room. She turned to Holy with her brows knit together. Should she take him to task for disrupting Bobby before he spilled Holy's last name? Or would that be unfair?

"Where did we leave off, Holy?" she said.

"I was about to ask you, how many of the Harpers were in on poisoning Slayter?"

"Guess." She grinned. "After all, you only have six names to deal with, unlike an infinity of last names that go very well with a man that has the first name of Holy."

"Touché, Elizabeth." Holy straightened his tie. "You probably only recruited one of the Harpers to help you poison Slayter. That person would be Grandma Harper. Am I right?"

"What made you think I would implicate any of my family, especially my grandma?"

"Each family member liked Slayter, but he came up with logical reasons for everyone to help poison him, except for Grandma. Maybe Grandma knew something they didn't?"

"You are partially correct. Grandma knew I was upset and made me confide in her."

"Confide, how?"

"I told her how much I loved Slayter, but he did some things that I could never condone."

"Did you include poisoning the poor lad to teach him a lesson?"

"No. Grandma is one tough cookie. How do you think she put up with Grandpa all these years? She never would have approved of my poisoning Slayter. Hitting him over the head with a frying pan, yep. Poisoning him, no. But she provided some salient advice."

"I can't wait to hear what she told you," Holy said.

"Grandma said, 'If Slayter Jones didn't rob a bank or kill someone, and you are really in love with him, then hit the son of a bitch with a frying pan so he'll never do what he did again, and then forgive him.'"

"So you are saying none of your family was in on the poisoning. And now I know how Grandma Harper kept Grandpa Harper in line."

"Correct on both accounts," she said. "As far as my family was concerned, Slayter was sick from some kind of stomach ailment. Actually, that was the truth. They all felt sorry for him, except for Grandpa. He thought Slayter was acting like a sissy."

"Slayter was really suffering. Didn't you feel a smidgeon sorry for him? After all, even if you were deeply disappointed in him, he was the person you wanted to spend the rest of your life with. At the very least, shouldn't you have confronted Slayter in person before sentencing him based on hearsay?"

"What can I say?" She winced. "My broken heart overruled all of my affection for him."

"Based on the lies you were told, I can understand why you did what you did, I just don't approve of how you did it. What I don't get is why Slayter would head back to Warren's house when time was such a critical issue?"

"I don't have to guess to answer that question. Slayter knew he had no chance of getting the antidote from me without his wallet."

Chapter Twenty (1955 Thanksgiving Day)

Three things were missing when Slayter dashed back into Warren's house. All traces of mud he tracked in earlier had been cleaned up. His filthy clothes were no longer lying on the bedroom floor where he had left them, and his wallet was probably in the washing machine along with his clothes. One wash cycle would ruin most of the contents in his billfold and any chance he had to convince Betsy not to hate him.

Slayter headed for the doorway. He'd been in such a hurry to clean up, he didn't think to empty his pockets. If he was lucky, maybe his dirty clothes were in a pile waiting to be washed. If not, the condition of his soggy wallet would dictate who he would see next.

Something caught his eye on the way to the doorway making him stop and stand like a statue. Was it a wishful-thinking mirage? Squinting, he moved to the dresser. The closer he got, the faster his heart pulsed. There was no mistaking his beat-up brown leather wallet sitting on top of the dresser. As horrible as Rhoda was in the kitchen, she was meticulous about cleaning the house, doing dishes, and washing clothes. This wasn't the first time she had saved his wallet from washing machine annihilation. He had every intention of giving her a heartfelt thank you before leaving the house. As he entered the hallway, sounds of loud passion emanating from behind the master bedroom door caught his ear. Perhaps Rhoda would appreciate his words of gratitude at a later time...if there was a later time for him.

Back inside his Bug, he sped to the Harper's place with his dry wallet stuffed securely in his back pocket. Rain had ceased for the moment. Eddie was following Doody who was tailing Slayter. They were a few vehicles short of a parade, but the night was still young.

As much as Slayter wanted to see Betsy, what were his chances of winning her over with or without his wallet? Would she even open the door? Maybe Mr. and Mrs. Harper wouldn't allow Betsy to see him even if she was willing. Maybe they would send Grandma Harper to the door armed with her favorite frying pan. A smiling Mr. Harper had once told Slayter that he was an avid hunter who never fired warning shots. Maybe her dad had been kidding. Or maybe he had given Slayter a heads-up warning.

The Harper house was a block away. Second and third thoughts crept into Slayter's head. Perhaps he should have bypassed confronting Betsy and gone straight to Paige's apartment. The issue of time was becoming more critical for him every second; which meant it was too late to change course even if he had fourth and fifth thoughts.

The Lincoln and Cadillac were still in the circular driveway in front of the Harper house. He parked in the same place and rushed up the walkway to the porch. He could see his breath in the cold air. A black cat skittered past Slayter, making him jump to the side. The cat hid in the bushes next to the brick trim. Was the feline an omen? A sharp pain hit low in his stomach. This was a bad time to start being superstitious. Once he was on the porch, his eyes shifted from the doorbell to the metal door knocker. Which one would give him a better chance for a good reception? Slayter's head shook for a second time. He would have no chance if he just stood there trying to make a decision.

Slayter knocked on the door with his knuckles. He waited for a response, then knocked again, harder. Same result. Was the entire Harper family huddled together inside the entryway, pointing at the door and guessing how long the poor schmuck on the porch would keep knocking before leaving? He aimed a forefinger at the doorbell. His finger was in midair when the door opened wide enough to stretch the chain lock. A strip of entryway light shined on him, but he had no way of knowing who was behind the door. Nor could he catch sight of a rifle or a frying pan. Every thoughtful argument he had rehearsed on the drive to the house disappeared from his head.

"We weren't expecting to see you again tonight, Slayter," Mr. Harper said, showing his face through the opening. "I assume you are feeling better."

"Much better, Mr. Harper. I apologize if I ruined everyone's Thanksgiving. I wouldn't have come back, except I need to talk to Betsy about an urgent matter."

"Uh…I don't think she wants to talk to you right now, Slayter." Mr. Harper cleared his throat. "After you left, she ran crying into her room. I don't make a habit of getting mixed up in my daughter's love life, but did you two have a fight or something?"

"Or something. It's imperative that I speak to Betsy."

"I don't know, Slayter. Honestly, I've never seen my daughter so distraught. Maybe you should give her a day or two."

"I don't have a day or two." Slayter's tone oozed desperation. He could hear ticking again. "Please, Mr. Harper. I wish I could explain it to you, but my time is running out."

Mr. Harper's tongue made a clicking sound as he considered Slayter's response. "I'll try, but I doubt it's going to do any good."

The door shut, leaving Slayter in the dark. Obviously, they weren't expecting him since the porch light was off. Or maybe they wanted him to take a hint in case he returned to the house. He twisted around to face the street. Doody's truck was parked at the curb. The walkie-talkie covered his mouth. Eddie's patrol car was idling behind the truck.

Slayter made a fist and punched it into his palm. What if Mr. Harper didn't return to give him an answer? How long should he wait? He studied the massive wooden front door. Was he desperate enough to try and bust the door down? He leaned a shoulder hard into the wood to test it. The only thing he would break was his shoulder.

He went back to punching his hand until the flesh screamed for mercy from the constant pummeling. If the door was unlocked, except for the chain lock, he could easily break the chain. He tried the door handle. It wouldn't budge. He was back to square one with the dice loaded against him. In "Monopoly" terms, he couldn't pass "Go" and collect $200.

Slayter switched punching hands. What if he went around to the side of the house and knocked on Betsy's bedroom window? He stepped off the porch to get a better look at the gate. He noticed Doody reading *Lolita* again with the cab light on. It would serve him right if his battery went dead. Officer Eddie was talking into his squad car radio. Slayter checked out the gate. He couldn't recall if the Harpers had a vicious dog in their backyard. There wasn't a

"Beware of Dog" warning sign anywhere to be found. How receptive would Betsy be if she saw him outside her bedroom window? What if she was undressing? Officer Eddie wouldn't have to go far to arrest him as a Peeping Tom. Worse yet, Mr. Harper wouldn't need a scope on his rifle to shoot him without a warning shot.

Slayter moved back onto the porch again and stared at the door. Something brushed against his ankle making his body flinch into the stucco wall. Percy the Pig flashed in his head. The purring black cat was rubbing its side back and forth on Slayter's leg, probably to make sure he got a double dose of bad luck.

He looked at his bare wrist again. Old habits die hard. How much longer should he stay? How much time did he have left before the temporary antidote would wear off? Would Betsy come to the door, or would Mr. Harper return to give him Betsy's answer? Should he knock on the door again?

"Hey, Slayter." Doody stood in the walkway waving the walkie-talkie. "Dr. Sinn wants to know what you are up to. You've been out front here for a long time."

"Tell Dr. Sinn I'm trying to earn my Boy Scout Merit Badge by doing a good deed. What the hell do you think I'm doing?"

"Dr. Sinn, Slayter says he's trying to earn his—"

Slayter jumped off the porch and grabbed the walkie-talkie. If Doody was his attorney representing him in court, he could envision himself being strapped to an electric chair.

"Listen, Dr. Sinn," Slayter shouted. "I've done everything you've asked of me. There's a good chance Betsy won't come to the door. You've got to tell me who has the antidote before I run out of time? Is it Betsy or is it Paige? *Over*!"

"Give me a second to formulate a suitable answer to your question." Static blasted from the speaker. "Why are you limiting your choices to Paige and Betsy? Couldn't Rhoda and Larry also have the antidote? *Over*."

"Doody and Rhoda swore they don't have the antidote. *Over*."

"Are you sure? What if one of them is lying? If Doody and Rhoda were telling you the truth, how do you know Betsy or Paige won't lie to you? Before today, you considered yourself to be a good judge of character. Now you don't know for sure if you can rely on any of the people you are seeking. Your clock is ticking, Mr. Jones. *Over and out*."

"Dr. Sinn, you answered my question with additional questions. Would it kill you to help me just a little?" It took every bit of Slayter's restraint not to smash the radio on the cement. "Maybe it won't kill you, but it sure might kill me. Thanks for nothing. *Over*!"

Did Dr. Sinn throw Slayter a bunch of red herrings to confuse him? He flipped the walkie-talkie in the air. Doody juggled it before grasping the radio with both hands and cradled it like a baby as he slinked back to the truck talking to himself.

Slayter advanced up to the porch and hammered a fist on the front door. No response. He banged his forehead against the hard wood, giving him a thumping headache and still no reply. Breathing hard, he left his forehead on the cool door while placing his palms flat on the wood as if he was about to scale a wall.

The door inched open until the chain lock caught. Slayter lost his balance, banging his forehead again. His eyelids blinked nonstop as he stepped back to focus on the narrow opening. Instead of seeing a long metal gun barrel or a frying pan project through the doorway, he observed a small trembling hand.

"You forgot the watch I gave you for your birthday on the counter in the guest bathroom," Betsy said in a weak voice. "Or did you leave it there as a subtle message?"

Slayter stared at the watch in her hand. Did she really want him to have it? Or was this a ploy to make him feel guiltier? He did feel responsible for the anguish she was going through, but not for the lies others had told her.

"I didn't leave the watch in the bathroom on purpose if that is what you were asking?" He reached for the watch, but he thought better of it. "Betsy, please let me explain."

"Slayter, there's nothing you can say to me that will change my mind," Betsy announced in a firm voice. She extended her arm out an inch. "Take your watch and go away. I never want to see you again."

"That watch was the nicest gift anyone has ever given to me because it came from you. I cherish that watch. Do you remember why you gave it to me?"

"That doesn't matter anymore," she choked out.

"On the contrary, the reason you gave me the watch is all that matters."

Her silence sent a loud message. He stared at the watch, not knowing what else to say.

"I gave you the watch," she said, "because it represented our *time* spent together and how much I *loved* being with you. I now realize how incredibly naïve I've been after learning our relationship on your part was based only on my doing research for your novel."

"That's not true, Betsy," Slayter said. "And I can prove it if you will give me a chance."

More silence. If he was in Betsy's place standing behind the door hurting beyond compare, would he be willing to listen to the person on the porch?

"There's nothing you can say or do that will make me feel different," she said.

Slayter reached into his back pocket and removed his wallet. Their fingertips touched sending him a jolt of pleasure when he snatched the watch. With his other hand, like a magician, he replaced the watch with his wallet. Betsy manipulated the leather with her fingers until she realized what she was holding.

"You've got to be kidding me," she said. "You're giving me your wallet. Is this a bribe to buy back my affection for you? Jeez, Slayter, take your wallet before I throw it at you."

"No. I'm trying to show that you have been deceived, but not by me. In the section where greenbacks are supposed to be stored, you won't find any money. I spent all of my cash on the bottle of wine I brought to your family's Thanksgiving. Instead, you will find a folded piece of paper. Keep the wallet – it's of no use to me now. If you promise to read what is on that piece of paper, I'll leave."

Betsy's hand remained outside the door holding his wallet as he waited for her to respond to his challenge. What other choice did he have? He held his breath, sorry he couldn't see her. This was probably the last opportunity he would ever get.

Chapter Twenty-One (1955 Thanksgiving Day)

Another cloudburst sent sheets of raindrops bombarding down on Bobsville, dampening Slayter's spirits even more. The drain spouts near to the Harper front porch gushed out streams of water into the garden. The porch overhang shielded him from the downpour, but not from the earsplitting noise. It felt like he was standing in the middle of a thundering war zone with both sides sending artillery back and forth.

Betsy's arm remained extended through the door's slim opening while she held his wallet in her hand. Slayter's eyes continued to be fixed on the wallet until it became a blur. What was Betsy waiting for? Was she undecided about what she should do? That would be a semi-positive sign. Or was she waiting for him to take back his wallet and leave? He resisted his desire to touch her silky-soft hand again.

A bolt of lightning cracked and rumbled, illuminating the sky like a giant lamp. The black cat that had startled him earlier brushed against his leg before scooting into the house through the doorway gap. Slayter had no control of the weather or what Betsy would do next. All he could do was wait, but for how long?

He leaned closer to the door. Did he hear a voice coming from inside the house? If so, it had to be Betsy's voice. The frail chain lock that stretched to its maximum was the only object keeping him from seeing her. He could easily break the chain apart by pounding his shoulder into the door, but Betsy would take the brunt of the blow. He was almost certain he heard a voice, but the rain's racket made the words impossible to decipher. Or was his mind playing a cruel trick on him?

"Betsy, were you talking to me?" he yelled. "I couldn't hear what you were saying."

Slayter strained to listen. Does straining to hear someone or something actually enhance one's hearing? Could she even hear what he had shouted as forcefully as he could?

"I said, if I take your wallet, will you please leave me alone, Slayter?" Betsy yelled back.

He could hear what she said loud and clear - too loud and too clear.

"Betsy, I'll leave if you promise to read what is on that piece of paper inside my wallet."

Slayter leaned his ear near the opening again. If she responded to him, he couldn't hear it.

"I will probably regret this," Betsy hollered.

She removed her arm and slammed the door forcefully in his face. It felt like the cover to his coffin had just been sealed. He waited a few beats, and then looked down at the doormat wondering what his next move would be. What did Betsy mean by "regret this?" Was she considering his request? Slayter smacked the side of his head the same way Doody often did. Betsy never promised to read the words he had carefully printed on the paper. There was no guarantee she would ever respond to him again. Did she take the wallet just to get rid of him? Yet, if he didn't leave now, it would give her another reason to disbelieve him.

He stepped back from the door. His jaw tightened. She never mentioned the antidote. Was that a positive or a negative sign? If she had the antidote, wouldn't she have said something like, "*If I take your wallet and give you the antidote, will you leave me alone?*" Had Betsy's feelings changed so much she would deny him the opportunity to undo the effects of the poison? If that was the case, he had lost something just as valuable as the antidote. He could only hope that someday Betsy would learn the truth.

Slayter attempted to stare through layers of rain. He could make out fuzzy visions of Doody and Eddie in their vehicles. Since Betsy refused to cooperate, what other choice did he have but to confront Paige at her apartment? If he departed now and discovered Paige didn't have the antidote, would there be enough time to come back to the Harper house and make a last-ditch plea at convincing Betsy she was his last hope? What were the chances she would change her tune about seeing him if he did come back?

Slayter fought through the driving wind and rain and headed to the Volkswagen. Doody repositioned himself behind his steering wheel. Eddie, on the other hand, was pointing a finger at Slayter, moving it back and forth as if sending a coded message. Slayter changed his course and worked his way to the squad car's passenger side. Eddie continued the finger pointing exercise until Slayter shook his head. That prompted Eddie to slide over on the bench seat and crank the handle that rolled down the window.

"I don't know what this means." Slayter said, mimicking Eddie's finger movement.

"Turn around, Slayter."

Was Eddie Rose playing games with him? Slayter rotated his body, turning his back to the patrol car. The front door was wide open. The porch light shined down on Betsy standing in the doorway still holding his wallet.

Slayter scampered to the porch. Water dripped off of him, forming a puddle around his shoes on the bricks. He couldn't help but shake from the cold. Or was the shiver from trepidation of what Betsy might do or say? She had changed into pink pedal pushers, blue sweatshirt, and blue fuzzy slippers. Her watery eyes were red from crying. A golf ball sized lump lodged in his throat. He had never seen her cry before.

Betsy made no attempt to return his wallet. Did she read what he had penned on the folded paper? Her head moved to the side as if something else had caught her attention.

"Why is Doody's truck parked in front of the house? And why is a police car parked behind him? Is Doody getting a ticket?"

"Unfortunately, no," Slayter said. "But Doody should be arrested for lying to you."

"Isn't that like the pot accusing the kettle of...whatever the pot was guilty of doing?" Her lips scrunched into an amusing expression. "I don't think I said that correctly. What I was trying to say, Slayter, you are the last person who should be criticizing someone for lying when you are at fault for deceiving a number of people who really cared about you."

"I realize you have lost all faith in me," he said. "Which probably means you won't allow yourself to consider anything I say. But if you would please hear me out, this may be the last chance I get to disprove the lies you were told."

Betsy shot a glare at him that would sober up the Bobsville town drunk. At least she hadn't thrown his wallet back at him.

"You believed the false stories Doody told you," Slayter said. "But your expression tells me you aren't open to hear my version. What do you think Doody would say to you with me standing here?" Betsy answered with a blank expression. "The problem is, Doody most likely won't get out of his truck if I ask him to join us. But if *you* signal for him to come to the porch, he will get here lickety-split. If you want to know the truth, Betsy, all you have to do is look Doody square in the eye and ask him if he lied to you about me. I have no doubt his answer will be different than what he said before."

Could Betsy tell he wasn't anywhere near as confident as his bold statement? At this point in the game, it was go bold or fold. Slayter was betting all of his chips that Doody's crush on Betsy would pressure him to come clean and tell the truth.

"If Doody acknowledges he lied to me," she said, "what does that prove, Slayter? He's your childhood buddy. Like everyone else in Bobsville, he would do anything for you." She waved the wallet. "Or maybe your presence will frighten him into thinking you will beat him up if he says the wrong thing. Can't you just admit what you did was wrong?"

"If four people came to me saying horrible things about you, Betsy, do you think for one second I'd believe them? No way. I'd tell each and every one of them to go fly a kite in a storm with a metal key attached. Then I would ask you if the lies they were spreading had any merit at all. But you didn't do that. Instead of coming to me, you believed their lies."

"That's your defense? To hold me responsible after they backed up each other's stories."

"I'm not blaming you," Slayter said. "You gave everyone a chance to confirm their stories, except me. It's not your fault each person had a different agenda against me. One lie developed into a series of lies. For what it's worth, I deserve blame for allowing people to enable me all of my life, but not for the lies you have been told."

Betsy shook her head. She reached for the door handle, then closed the door behind her. She motioned with a forefinger for Doody to join them. Doody, minus the walkie-talkie and *Lolita*, sprinted to the porch like he was about to be presented a prize. He made sure to stand several arm lengths away from Slayter.

"I apologize in advance, Doody, for asking you this question," she said. "Did you lie to me about Slayter?"

Doody shook his head. "Nope."

Slayter almost swallowed his Adam's apple. His gamble had backfired when Doody called his bluff, whether it was intentional or not. Did Doody even realize he was signing Slayter's death warrant?

"You told me Slayter was sleeping with Paige, isn't that correct, Doody?" Betsy said.

"That's rightsville." Doody smiled at Betsy but moved another step away from Slayter.

"You were privy to this information because Paige said they were sleeping together?"

"Privy?" Doody bit down on his lip. "Paige didn't say nothing about bathrooms when she done told me about her and Slayter. But no lie, it came straight from her mouth."

"How do you know if Paige was telling you the truth?" Betsy asked.

"It had to be true 'cause Paige told me so. If anyone would know, it would be her."

Slayter couldn't hold back any longer. "If Paige told you that Betsy is a communist spy sent by the Soviet Union, would you believe her?"

"Nah," Doody said with a chuckle. "Come on, Slayter. Betsy's no commie."

"If it came straight from Paige's mouth, Doody, then Betsy is a communist spy, right?"

Doody's mouth opened, but no words flew out. He aimed a finger in the air, changed his mind and pointed at Slayter. Then his features brightened as if a light bulb turned on.

"But Paige didn't say that Betsy was a Russian spy," Doody said.

"Doody," Betsy said in a soft voice. "Did you make up the story about Slayter just using me to do research for his book?"

Doody's cheeks colored the same shade as his hair. "I...ah...well that wasn't exactly a lie. People is always doing things for Slayter. He uses everybody."

"Yes, I'm well aware of that," Betsy said. "Let me put it another way. Did Slayter ever say to you he pretended to be my friend to use me to do his research?"

"Well, not exactly to me." Doody's eyes widened. "But Slayter could have said it to someone else. It's possible, right?"

"Good evening, ma'am," Eddie said, standing on the walkway in the pouring rain. "Is there a problem here?"

"Yes, officer," Betsy said. "We have a major problem, but it's not worthy of police involvement. We were just trying to settle a big difference in opinion."

"Eddie Rose, please meet Betsy Harper," Slayter said. "You, of course, know Doody."

Eddie tipped his hat to Betsy and flashed a flirty smile. Betsy smiled back.

"Actually, Miss Harper, we've met once before," Eddie said. "You caught a youngster stealing a book from the library and wanted to teach him a lesson. So you called the police department. I was the officer that gave the lad a stern warning about what would happen to him if he ever swiped anything again."

"I'm sorry, Officer Rose." she said. "I didn't recognize you with your hat on. You did such a great job scaring that boy, he ended up re-shelving books at the library for extra credit at school."

"Are you in need of my assistance again, Miss Harper?" Eddie asked.

"Not at the moment, Officer Rose. But I sure appreciate the offer."

"It's nice to make your acquaintance again, Miss Harper." Eddie tipped his hat and left.

"Any chance you changed your mind about going on a date with me?" Doody asked.

"I'm sorry, Doody. I'm going to say no again. This time for an entirely different reason. But thank you for asking."

A dejected Doody slinked away without the prize he coveted. Slayter had not one ounce of pity for him. At least Doody still had *Lolita*.

Slayter rubbed his forehead. What was wrong with this picture? He got poisoned for doing nothing wrong. Yet Doody lied to Betsy and got a sweet thank you.

"It's obvious that Doody lied to you," Slayter said. "So did Paige and Rhoda."

"Yes, I get why Doody would want to sully your reputation with me, but I'm not convinced Paige was lying, Slayter. Same with Rhoda. Why would Paige say she was having an affair with you if she wasn't? Girls just don't go around bragging about having sex with someone, even if that someone is the irresistible Slayter Jones. And why would Rhoda lie about you making sexual advances?"

"I found out tonight why Rhoda created the lie she told you," Slayter said. "She wanted me out of the house so she could have Warren all to herself. So that she could turn my room into a baby's room. She was wrong about deceiving you, Betsy, but I should have had the sense to move out after they got married."

"What about Paige?" Betsy asked.

"Paige's lie was the seed that started all the ill feelings about me. I have no idea why she would make up something like that, but I'm determined to find out."

"You know why Rhoda and Doody lied, but not Paige. Could it be because you are guilty of what she accused you of doing and lying to me?"

Betsy reached into his wallet, found the folded piece of paper, and crumbled it up.

Chapter Twenty-Two (1955 Thanksgiving Day)

Slayter's tennis shoe failed to trap the wind-driven paper ball on his first attempt. A second try captured his pathetic strategy to win Betsy back by stomping on it with his shoe. He never felt uncomfortable in Betsy's presence before tonight, but the wall of tension between them was so thick, famous strongman Charles Atlas wouldn't have been able break through it.

Betsy handed Slayter his wallet, then she rubbed her hands over her sweatshirt sleeves. The porch overhang sheltered them from the rain, but not the biting cold. Yesterday he would have placed cordial arms around her to provide warmth that would take her chill away. He jammed the wallet into his pocket, then draped his coat over her shoulders. He was out of jackets and almost out of time.

"You don't have to be nice to me anymore, Slayter," she said. "All of the research for your book is done."

"Come on, Bets. You know our relationship wasn't based on your ability to do research."

"That's the problem, Slayter. I thought I knew you. Obviously, I didn't. Or I had blinders on." A line etched between Betsy's brows. "For your information, I didn't poison you."

"How could you poison me? I didn't have anything to eat at your house."

"What I meant was I didn't put my portion of Dr. Sinn's concoction in your food."

Now Slayter knew why Dr. Sinn had said, "I'm surprised you're not in worse shape, Mr. Jones." The doctor assumed he had ingested all three doses of his Thanksgiving poison.

"What stopped you, Betsy?"

"When I opened the door earlier, all it took was one look at you to know that Paige and Rhoda had tainted your meals. I just couldn't make myself do it. You were so sick, I wasn't sure what you needed more - a hospital or Yoo Mortuary." She threw her hands in the air. "I felt sorry for you, okay, not that I should have. And maybe it's also because..."

Betsy turned her head away from him. She gulped for air and waited to regain her breath. When she faced him again, lines of tears stained her cheeks.

"In spite of the way you hurt me, how could I poison the man I was in love with?"

"Wow." Slayter's head jolted back. Words he longed to hear from her, but not like this.

"I wasn't sure how deep your feelings were for me," Slayter said. "You never gave me any indication of wanting our relationship to be anything more than just best of friends. I figured you might be waiting for your Mr. Right to come along. Or maybe you were waiting for a guy you had a crush on to finally notice you."

"I did have a crush on someone, Slayter. You were my Mr. Right. For a smart guy, you can really be clueless. How could you not know I was in love with you?"

"You could have given me some kind of hint," he said, lifting his shoulders into his neck.

"Didn't it occur to you I didn't date anyone after you walked into the library asking for research help on your novel? *Hint.* I specifically asked if you were seeing someone, and you said no. *Hint. Hint.* We spent almost all of our free time with each other. *Hint. Hint. Hint.* Didn't it ever come to mind even once that we were, in a very real sense, going together as a couple? *Hint. Hint. Hint. Hint.*"

"Well, yes, but not exactly in those words. Betsy, our relationship was so perfect I didn't want to take a chance of ruining anything if you didn't feel the same way about me."

"How do I know you aren't just saying that because you think I have the antidote? After all, you lied to me about Paige. I can't express how much it hurt when I heard what was going on between the two of you."

"I never lied to you about anything, including Paige," he said. "And I know you don't have the antidote. If you did, you would have offered it to me by now – for the same reason you didn't poison me.

That means Paige is the only person who could have the antidote." He stooped to pick up the wad of paper and squeezed it in his palm. "The time Dr. Sinn gave me is running out, but I can't leave yet. Even if you won't read this, I can still prove my feelings for you have never changed, if you will let me."

Betsy locked eyes with him. She didn't say no. That was as good as a yes.

"Slayter, there is something you should know about the antidote. It's not—"

"Betsy," Slayter interrupted, "you are the only person, besides Paige, who has read all the typed first draft pages of *What If?*. You know it leaves off where my protagonist, Hunter, is standing at the crossroads of his life deciding which road he should take. His special power of being able to foresee the future reveals his destiny for all three directions. The road to his left would send him to a highly successful career he has coveted over everything, including love. The road to his right would lead him to an exciting political shady-side-of-the-law life of fame and fortune. And the road in the middle would guide him to the woman he will love forever even though their life together will be filled with hardships and poverty. What road do you think Hunter will choose?"

"I don't know," she said. "You never told me or anyone how your story ended. For the sake of secrecy, I understood why you didn't share your ending, but I have to admit I was disappointed you wouldn't trust me."

"The reason I didn't tell you had nothing to do with trust. I wanted to surprise you. It was my subtle way of showing how I felt about you. If Hunter chose the road leading to a life of love, do you remember the name of the woman?"

"How could I forget? Her name is Elizabeth. No one ever calls me by my given name except Grandma Harper."

"The character, Elizabeth, was named after you. Hunter pursued the road that would lead him to Elizabeth, knowing full well he could never be satisfied with his other futures of thrills and prosperity without her in it - the same way I feel, and have always felt, about you, Betsy. This isn't how I envisioned springing it on, but you are now the only other person who knows how the story ends."

Slayter held out his hand. "Do believe me."

"I don't know what to believe." She stared at the crumpled ball of paper. "How would I know for sure if whatever is on that piece of paper is true or not? Nor do I know when you wrote it. You could have created it this evening as a way to cover your behind."

Slayter blew out an exasperated breath. Betsy was determined not to read what was on the paper. How could he convince her to believe him?

"Do you remember when we went to see the new animated movie *Lady and the Tramp* earlier this year? At the ticket booth, I reached into my wallet, removed a dollar bill and a folded piece of paper fell out. In fact, you picked up the paper and handed it to me. I quickly put the paper back into my wallet. You looked at me kind of funny and then accused me of trying to hide something from you. Do you recall what I said?"

"Sort of." She peered up at the porch ceiling. "I can't remember your exact words, but you said something like, what is written on this piece of paper was meant for me and hopefully you would be able show it to me in the near future."

"Close enough," he said. "At any rate, this scrunched up piece of paper I'm holding in my hand is the same piece of paper you retrieved for me at the movies."

Betsy removed the paper ball from his palm. She gazed at it as if there might be a special way of unfolding it without doing damage. Her fingers shook as she carefully stretched one layer at time, ironing out as many wrinkles as she could. When the printed message was exposed, her lips moved with each word. She gazed at Slayter, and then read it again.

"For goodness sakes, Elizabeth, will you please read it out loud before I catch my death of cold," Grandma Harper bellowed, standing in the doorway holding a frying pan.

"Shame on you, Grandma. These words are personal between Slayter and me."

"Well, if you won't, I will." Grandma Harper snatched the paper from Betsy's hand and squinted. "I didn't think to bring my reading peepers. It's kind of tough to see with all the creases, but it says,

'*WHAT IF?* IS DEDICATED TO BETSY HARPER, MY FOREVER BEST FRIEND AND LOVE OF MY LIFE.'"

"Kind of sappy." Grandma gave the paper back to Betsy and tapped Slayter's ass with the frying pan. "This man's a keeper. Make up with the poor guy and give him a smooch."

Grandma Harper mumbled something incoherent and closed the door, leaving them alone. Betsy refolded the note the exact way Slayter had. Then she threw her arms around his neck and kissed him the way a woman would kiss the man she was going with.

"What took you so long?" Slayter placed two fingers under her chin.

"I have been waiting for you to make the first move since the day you walked into the library and asked me to help you research your novel."

"Does this mean I would never have to worry about you poisoning my meals for the next fifty years?"

"Yes!" She kissed him again. "I'm so sorry, Slayter. I was wrong not to trust you. Please, let me go with you to Paige's apartment." She peered down at her slippers. "It won't take me more than a minute to get some shoes on and grab Grandma Harper's frying pan."

"As much as I always want you by my side," he said, "I have to complete this journey on my own before Dr. Sinn's temporary antidote wears off. Doctor's orders."

"Slayter, I've been trying to tell you—"

Slayter kissed her and dashed into the storm ready to travel a road he should have chosen first. He'd return to Betsy with the antidote and Paige's reason for lying – or die trying.

Chapter Twenty-Three (1955 Thanksgiving Day)

Slayter couldn't recall scurrying from the Harper porch through the rainstorm to his car. He settled in behind the steering wheel dripping wet. The last couple of minutes with Betsy had transformed his doldrums into near euphoria. She was back in his life – the best medicine of all. Even the paint canister driver's seat felt more comfortable.

The Bug's dashboard clock - which ran a tick or two slow - told him he had less than an hour before the temporary antidote would lose its potency. Betsy, Doody, and Rhoda had been eliminated from his search for the holy antidote, which could only mean Paige had possession of it. He pumped a confident fist in the air. He was on a roll. Nothing was going to stop him now from obtaining the remedy that would end his troubles.

Before he could turn the ignition key to engage the engine, a voice outside the open window stopped Slayter. Eddie's eyelids were working overtime to combat wind driven raindrops. He pulled the bill of his blue hat down as far as it would go. Did Eddie change his mind about being on Slayter's side?

"Didn't mean to startle you, Slayter," Eddie shouted. "The storm is causing all sorts of havoc around town. A call came over the radio to direct police, fire, and public works to areas where fallen trees, branches, and down electrical wires have created hazardous conditions." He took a quick look at the Harpers' lighted porch. "I'm surprised we still have electricity. It won't be long before we lose it. Sorry, man, but unless you need my assistance with the difficulty you're in, I'm gonna have to leave. From the looks of your interaction with Miss Harper on the porch, you're not having any trouble at all."

"I appreciate your help, Eddie. You're right. Everything seems under control now."

Eddie raised his head, then bent down again and touched

Slayter's shoulder. "Man, if you didn't know it already, you sure have great taste in chicks."

From the side mirror, Slayter watched Eddie's blurry form hightail it to Doody's truck. He couldn't tell if Doody was relaying a report into the walkie-talkie. Dr. Sinn's influence was still an issue since Paige was the only person left who would have the antidote. Hopefully, by now the doctor was aware that he was abiding by the rules.

Slayter gunned the Bug in the direction of Paige's apartment complex. His initial analysis was obviously flawed. In hindsight, he should have first gone to the person who turned everyone against him. Doody's headlights shined in Slayter's rearview mirror. Slayter made a sharp turn without braking, causing his car's back end to slide towards the curb. He was able to right his car and speed forward. Doody wasn't as fortunate. The truck skidded off the wet street and onto someone's front lawn.

All through the process of recording his novel for Paige, Slayter had been pleased with their working relationship. But there was something about her he never liked, yet he could never pinpoint what that something was until earlier today. Now he understood why she pushed him so hard to complete the first draft of his novel. And the reason why Paige became so upset when he wouldn't reveal how his story ended.

A sudden burst of hailstones pounded down on his car, blinding his vision of the road. It felt and sounded like his Bug was being bombarded with frozen bullets. Slayter had no choice but to pull over to the curb and wait for the hailstorm to subside. He couldn't tell if Doody did the same. Seconds were wasting away, and there was nothing he could do about it except try to figure out how he could get the antidote from Paige. He still didn't know why she would make up a story about sleeping with him. Why would she want to turn Betsy, Rhoda, and Doody against him? Or why she would risk losing a client? Slayter was dizzy from shaking his head. There was only one thing he was sure of – he had done something to turn her against him. Did he miss a clue or two from earlier in the day that might provide answers? He flashed back to his nerve-racking second Thanksgiving at Paige's apartment...

It took several minutes of coasting through Paige's apartment complex parking lot before he found an empty spot. The ache in his stomach had worsened. So had the loud and weird noises it was producing. It had to be something he ate. Maybe too many potato chips along with the Brussels sprouts Rhoda had prepared just for him at his first dinner? How the heck would he be able to down two more Thanksgiving meals?

He headed for the first floor lobby. His initial instinct had been to decline Paige's Thanksgiving invitation. He changed his mind when she threw in a teaser about something of vital importance they needed to discuss. He had no idea what she wanted to talk about or why they had to meet on Thanksgiving Day. This would be the first time they would break bread or drumsticks together. Maybe she had no one else to spend the day with? Hopefully her reason for meeting with him had everything to do with his novel.

Slayter left the bottle of wine he had purchased earlier on the front passenger seat. He spent every dollar he had in his wallet for a proper gift to give to Betsy's parents as a thank you for inviting him. This wouldn't be the first time he would visit with the Harper family, but being invited to a holiday meal was something special and the next phase in his relationship with Betsy. He didn't feel compelled to bring Paige a bottle of wine since it might give her a false impression about something other than his writing.

The rain had lightened. Walking fast was difficult in his condition. Paige's apartment was on the third and top floor of the building. He stopped. Something was wrong. There wasn't one light visible in the apartment windows. The power must be off. How long would Bobsville be without electricity? The hands on the wristwatch Betsy had given him illuminated in the darkness. He was sixteen minutes late.

Slayter moved as fast as he could into the lobby and waited for his eyes to adjust to the darkness. He stood in front of the only elevator, pushed the black button, and waited for a light to go on and a bell to ding. Then he realized there wouldn't be any light or ding without electricity. He placed a hand on his nauseous stomach. The last thing he wanted was a climb up two flights of stairs. He had a strong urge to turn around and go back to his car. His only motivation to stay was maybe Paige had good news about his novel. He moved to a door leading to the stairway. Halfway up to the second floor, he held onto the railing to regain his wind. The ache in his stomach had spread to his head.

Reaching the third floor landing, he closed his eyes and placed both hands on his thighs. He had made it up the stairs; now could he muster more steps to her apartment? The carpeted hallway was easier on him than walking up the cement stairs. He stood in front of Paige's door and leaned a shoulder against the wood. A desire to walk away as fast as he could was more and more appealing to him. He hoped he would be the only guest invited. If Paige had slaved through a day's worth of roasting a turkey with all the fixings, how upset would she get with his lack of appetite for food and to be social?

The door opened. The next thing Slayter knew, he was lying on her shag carpet. He turned over trying to get his eyes to focus. If falling down face first was a jolt to his system, seeing Paige after his eyes cleared was an even a bigger shock. She was wearing a long black sheer negligee.

"Thanks for dropping in, Slayter," she said. "That was quite an entrance."

"I didn't realize this was a pajama party." The fall didn't help Slayter's stomach, but Paige's outfit was momentarily soothing his discomfort.

"I told you to dress comfortably." She held out a hand to help him up. "I think we will be more comfortable on the couch."

His eyes surveyed the living room. Illumination came from flaming candlelight wherever there was a shelf or table, giving the room an eerie effect. The furniture blended well together, except for a television set enclosed in a black cabinet with brown covered speakers on each side. The dinette table at the back of the room was set for two, answering one of Slayter's questions. Taper candles were centered on the table.

Slayter rose to his feet in stages. He moved to sit on one end of the couch. Paige sat a few inches from him, much closer than she needed to be, adding to his discomfort.

"What did you want to discuss with me?" he asked. "It must be important if you chose a holiday to meet."

"Before we get to that, the power outage destroyed our Thanksgiving dinner. The turkey, stuffing, gravy...everything was ruined with the exception of one dish."

"I'm sorry, Paige. I wonder how many other homes are having the same problem."

Slayter's stomach belted out a noise Paige's neighbors could probably hear.

"Goodness, was that your stomach declaring its disappointment? Don't worry, Slayter, I promise you won't go home hungry or unsatisfied."

"Food is the last thing I'm concerned about at the moment. What did you want to talk to me about?"

"I think we make a damn good team together." She leaned closer to him. "Don't you?"

"Uh, sure," he said. "You've done a great job taking my story and formatting it into a novel. The amazing part is that you didn't change my writer's voice or the essence of my story. Do all editors have that ability?"

"Absolutely not," Paige shot back. "That's what I'm talking about, Slayter. I know you have more good stories in you. As a team, we could pump out book after book."

"Why do you need me to be a published author, Paige? You can do it on your own."

"Do you see that large black binder in the bookcase?" Paige said, pointing. "It's full of rejection letters. I don't have your creative gift." She moved closer to him. "Don't you get it? We complement each other. Why even think about it? We should be a team."

"We haven't finished What If? yet. How do you even know a publisher will take it?"

"What would you say if I told you a literary agent is interested in What If?"

"I would say that is unbelievable." His stomach pain was still present, but he felt a surge of energy. Was Paige jiving him to make a deal? "When did you talk to an agent?"

"The day I invited you to be my Thanksgiving guest." She put her hand on his knee. "I had sent the agent the first two chapters. He

requested the whole manuscript. Isn't that exciting? It means he's really interested, but I can't submit it to him unless you dictate to me how the story ends."

"Shouldn't you have talked to me first before sending my novel chapters to an agent?"

"Slayter, I was only acting as a pre-agent for you. Just testing the waters. I would think you would be grateful, especially considering the results."

"It's not that I'm not grateful, Paige. I just think you should have—"

The apartment lights suddenly came on. Slayter could hear Frank Sinatra singing "In the Wee Small Hours" on the hi-fi. A buzzer went off from the kitchen. Paige rolled her eyes and left Slayter to turn off the buzzer. On her return from the kitchen, she switched off the lights, stood in front of him, and took his hands into hers.

"Slayter, becoming a writing team should be a no-brainer for you," she said. "Instead of a handshake, let's consummate our partnership in the bedroom."

Before Slayter could answer, his stomach rumbled to its boiling point. He jumped up and headed for the first closed door he could find. Unfortunately, the door led to a bedroom.

"My, aren't you the eager beaver," Paige swooned. "That's my roommate Sally's bedroom, but it will do. She's visiting friends in San Francisco."

Slayter jumped back into the hallway, opened the next closed door, and entered the bathroom. Paige's hair products, bath salts, and lit candles were on the sides of a bathtub. A shower head protruded from the wall. Hopefully, he wouldn't need the tub, but the toilet with a fuzzy pink cover was in for a big challenge.

* * * * *

Slayter closed the bathroom door and wobbled towards the living room. He peeked into the kitchen. Only one pot was on a stove burner, otherwise there wasn't any sign of heavy duty Thanksgiving cooking. Paige stood by the dinette table when he returned.

"Sorry about that," he said. "It couldn't be helped."

"Perhaps it gave you time to reconsider our partnership agreement and all of its perks."

"For the time being, I'm going to decline, Paige. It's not that I don't appreciate your assertiveness and offer to be partners, but before I agree to anything with you, I want to share your partnership proposal with Betsy."

"What does Betsy know?" Paige fired back. "She's a librarian who provides research for you. That certainly doesn't make her knowledgeable about the publishing industry."

"Betsy is just as much a part of my book as you and I."

"Is your loyalty to her coming from your heart or your head? Please stop all of this foolishness and tell me your ending."

"At the moment, I'm in no condition or frame of mind to dictate it to you."

Paige's eyes narrowed. She looked towards the kitchen, then back at him. Her head nodded slightly, as if she had made a silent agreement with herself.

"I can't tell you how disappointed I am in you, Slayter," she said. "You're a smart guy. I believe if you take a few minutes more to consider what our union would create, you will change your mind. In the meantime, you must sample the dish I made special for you."

"It's not that I don't appreciate whatever you prepared for me, Paige. It's just a matter of my stomach—"

"I've never seen this side of you, Slayter. It's certainly not very becoming. Do you know how hurtful your behavior is? Or how ungrateful you seem? I'm not going to take no for an answer. Now, please sit down at the table so I can serve you."

Paige returned with the pot and a serving spoon. She scooped out a spoonful of Brussels sprouts that had the same tangy aroma as Rhoda's sprouts. Same recipe?

Chapter Twenty-Four (1955 Thanksgiving Day)

The hailstorm stopped as suddenly as it started, bringing Slayter back to present time. Tiny beads of mist sprinkled the windshield. A sense of calm restored, Slayter could hear himself breathe over his idling engine. He drove the Bug onto a street dotted with balls of ice that were destined to melt to death in a matter of minutes.

Slayter looked twice at his rearview mirror. Doody's truck remained at the curb. For whatever reason, Dr. Sinn's spy dog wasn't following him. Trying to figure out why Doody did something often caused brain fatigue. Instead, Slayter focused on trying to make up for lost time that the hailstorm had robbed from him by speeding to Paige's apartment complex.

His mouth twitched. If today was yesterday, when being enabled was still in vogue, he wouldn't have to face this dilemma. His life had been so much easier when he knowingly and unknowingly permitted people to do everything for him. His yesterdays were a bad habit that needed breaking. All he had to do was live through today. He didn't need a mirror to know his features were bunched together into an ugly mask. He never wanted to face another Brussels sprout or Thanksgiving dinner for the rest of his life – a life that was about to end unless he could convince Paige to give him the antidote. What was Dr. Sinn's reasoning to give Paige the antidote honors? Slayter understood why the doctor didn't offer the antidote to Doody, but why not assign it to Rhoda or Betsy?

Slayter switched the heater to the off position since it wasn't providing one snippet of warm air. His earlier experience with Paige in her apartment was mind boggling. She was like a different person. His first tip-off should have been the long black negligee that was meant to throw him off guard. It was a precursor of her ploy to seal the deal in her bedroom. She was determined to take advantage of his weakened condition, knowing Rhoda had fed him her portion of Dr. Sinn's potion. Paige had no intention of preparing a full Thanksgiving dinner for him. The small pot on the stove containing Brussels sprouts was her plan P for poison if he refused to partner up with her. Or maybe she would have served him the tainted sprouts just on general principle or downright meanness. His respect for Paige as an ally had changed dramatically. Now he was aware that Paige could be his enemy - but an adversary that he needed to respect.

Paige's apartment complex was a block and a half away. The antidote was the only advantage she had on him. That alone put him at a great disadvantage. He was still baffled about what he had done to make Paige turn against him. If he knew the answer to that question, it would most likely solve why she lied about having an affair with him. He had experienced braggadocious males who lied about their conquests, but he had never met a woman, especially one in her thirties, who flaunted her sexcapades. He was also having trouble figuring out why Paige had pushed him to team up with her. With a binder full of rejection letters, was she so desperate to get published that she needed a writing partner? Did she really have an agent interested in his novel? Or did she make that story up, too? He harkened back to when they first met to discuss editing and transforming his verbalized chapters onto paper. Paige emphasized every author she had ever worked with thought their story would become the next best-selling book in all forty-eight states. He couldn't help but smile at that insight since he felt the same as her other clients about his novel, *What If?*. What if Paige wouldn't give him the antidote unless he agreed to partner up with her? Had she reached that moment of total despair?

A familiar object appeared in the rearview mirror. Doody's truck had crept up to ride the Bug's back bumper. The truck followed Slayter into the complex parking area. He found the same parking space as before. Doody drove past him, then disappeared trying to find a vacant space of his own. Instead of heading to the lobby entrance, Slayter went out of his way to make sure Paige's car was in her parking spot. He changed course when he spotted her red Plymouth Belvedere convertible in its place with the white top up.

The whole apartment complex was dark when he had approached the lobby earlier. This time, most of the apartment windows emitted some semblance of light. Slayter heard Doody's truck, causing him to stop and turn around. Doody parked behind the Bug, thus ensuring Slayter wouldn't be able to take off without him.

Slayter entered the lobby. If Paige had the antidote, she should be expecting him. Would she still be wearing the stimulating long black negligee with a candlelit background? Or did she have more surprises in store for him? This time he would be ready for her. Failure would bring on no tomorrow for a man who had a lot to live for.

He felt well enough to run up the stairs but decided to conserve his energy. When the elevator door slid open, a young couple left the car carrying several Thanksgiving doggie bags. A whiff of fragrant food aromas made him hold his breath. He could only hope, for their sake, tangy-tasting Brussels sprouts weren't in any of the bags. The ride up to the third floor creaked and rocked. The car hopped before coming to a stop. Nervous energy made him speed-walk to Paige's apartment door. A nagging negative thought kept banging around in his brain: what would he do if Paige wouldn't answer her door? Break the door down? Yell and scream until her neighbors complained? Try to find his new cop friend Eddie Rose and ask him to use his influence to get Paige to open up?

He knocked harder on the door than usual. A knock that conveyed Slayter Jones had his strength back. He waited for what felt like an eternity and knocked again. She still didn't answer. He leaned an ear closer to the door but couldn't hear anything. He banged on the wood again. Same result. His hand formed into a fist to pound on the door with everything he had.

"Who's there?" Paige's voice filtered from inside the apartment.

Slayter stared at the door as if it had called him a dirty name. Paige had to know who it was. Or was Paige expecting another client? Was this a dual poison night?

"Paige, it's Slayter. Open the door."

He waited a few seconds before the door opened halfway. Paige stuck her head out, looked in both hallway directions and stepped back into the apartment. He moved inside and closed the door. The lights were on and the candles were nowhere in sight. She had changed into a dark blue dress dotted with white spots. The gown had a plunging neckline and the hem fell below her knees. Blue high heels left her an inch shorter than Slayter. Her dark, puffy hair and bright red lipstick were the same. Did she get all dolled up for him or did she have somewhere to go?

"Have you changed your mind about our becoming a writing team?" she asked.

"You know damn well why I came back, Paige," he growled. "Give me the antidote to the poison you and Rhoda put in the Brussels spouts."

"You didn't mention your little librarian friend Betsy. She was in on it, too. How do you know Betsy and the others don't have the antidote?"

"Because Doody, Rhoda, and Betsy denied having it." He looked around the apartment. Nothing had changed except there was a manila folder on the dinette set next to her purse. "They also said they would give the antidote to me if they had it. I believed them."

"What if I told you Dr. Sinn didn't give me the antidote?" She batted her lashes.

"I wouldn't believe you."

"I was expecting that answer." Paige smirked. "For the sake of time, let's say Sinn did entrust me with the antidote. What are you willing to give me for it in return, Slayter?"

Slayter's jaw dropped. If possible, Paige was more demented than Dr. Sinn. Was that the reason the doctor gave Paige the antidote; one crazy understanding the other crazy? At least Dr. Sinn took part in their scheme to teach Slayter a valuable lesson. Paige, conversely, was using the antidote as a bargaining chip to get what she wanted, as well as teaching him a lesson about trust.

"How do you know I won't physically force you to give me the antidote?" he said.

"If you haven't attempted to manhandle me by now, you won't. Face it, Slayter, you're not the type of person who would rough up a woman. To prove that point, there was a scene in your novel where your protagonist, Hunter, had every right to beat the living daylights out of a deserving woman, but he didn't. When I suggested the scene would work better if Hunter got physical with the woman, you refused my critique by maintaining the act was morally repulsive to you even in a story of fiction." Paige put her hands on her shapely hips. "By the way, if you lay one hand on me, I will scream *rape* as loud as an air raid siren. You should be getting the big picture of me by now – when I'm engaged in a negotiation for something, I throw morals aside. Hence, I offered you my body, but you turned me down. Believe me, that was a new experience. Was it because you are shagging that prissy librarian, Betsy, and you want to be faithful to her?"

"Are you serious, Paige? Come back to Realsville. We're talking about someone's life here. My life. Please give me the antidote before it's too late."

"What is it worth to you, Slayter?"

Slayter's fuse was about to blow. A smirk appeared on Paige's painted lips again. And why not? She was holding the antidote. He had spent his whole life in a world of naïveté. If he had taken the time and effort to write the story that had been in his head for years, instead of hiring Paige to do the chore, he wouldn't be in this predicament. If nothing else he had learned this Thanksgiving, his habit of being dependent on others when it wasn't necessary handicapped his ability to function and progress. In a sense, he was fortunate this was a defect that could be corrected, if he could only endure the current crisis.

Paige wrapped her arms around herself and tapped a shoe in the carpet. She was losing patience with him. He had no choice but to give in to her.

"What do you want in return for the antidote, Paige?" Slayter asked.

"It's too bad you are so selfish. I gave you a chance, and you didn't take it. Therefore, my generous offer of partnership is now off the table. That was a very bad move on your part, Slayter, because now I've upped the stakes. I want the epiphany, result, and ending to the novel."

Slayter could hear ticking in his head again. Paige just answered one of his questions; an agent was interested in his story; a compliment that would have overjoyed him yesterday. Did Paige want his ending so bad she was willing to let him die if she couldn't get it?

"I will tell you how the story ends in return for the antidote," he said. "But first, why did you lie to Doody about me sleeping with you?"

"Not so fast, slick. You get nothing from me until I get what I want."

"What's the matter, Paige? You essentially said I was too moral for my own good. Now you don't trust me? Some partner you would have made. Think about it. If I don't get the antidote soon, you will get nothing. Tell me why you lied."

"You made another serious mistake by telling me you shared all of the finished *What If?* chapters with Betsy. I explicitly told you not to tell anyone anything about your novel until I said it was ready. Some partner *you* would have made."

"Paige, allow me to remind you that you were hired and paid to transcribe and edit my story. That doesn't give you the right to own any of my work."

"Correction, there is no record of you being the author. The transcribed chapters I returned to you only have my name on them because I'm the author of *What If?*.

"My brother Warren paid you. That, alone, is proof of ownership."

"How do you know Warren paid me?" she said. "He would be hard pressed to show any payment to me or anyone else since he paid in cash, just as I requested. And I don't show any record of receiving payment from Warren for my services. Furthermore, there is no signed contract. No paperwork in your name or mine. That means the novel *What If?* belongs to me. After all, you didn't write it, I did. When it gets published, my name will be on the front cover in big letters, and my picture will grace the back cover. The only person you can blame is yourself. You brought the librarian into the picture and then rejected my offer of dual authorship. Like I said before, Slayter, bad moves on your part."

Slayter closed his eyes and rubbed the back of his head. How could he be so careless? So naïve. Paige lied to alienate Betsy against him and force her out of the picture. Paige's plan would have worked perfectly if he hadn't told Paige that Betsy was privy to his chapters. His slip of the tongue changed everything.

"The ending is yours, Paige." He could hear his heart thumping. "Show me the antidote."

"It pleases me to no end that you are finally seeing things my way," she said, pointing a finger at the dining table. "But first you are going to sign and date a document inside that manila folder that says you have read Paige Turner's work of fiction entitled *What If?*.

"I won't sign anything until you show me the antidote."

Paige nodded. She walked to the table, removed a small glass vial from her purse, and jiggled the container. Several pills rattled around inside.

"Let me see the antidote," he said.

Paige poured out seven white capsules onto the table, emptying the container.

"Before you ask, Slayter, one of the capsules is Dr. Sinn's antidote. The others are placebos, which in your case is a deadly poison. Lucky for you, I know the difference. It's my 'Break Glass In Case of an Emergency' backup, just in case you aren't as honorable as I thought.

"How do I know you will give me Dr. Sinn's antidote?"

"Once you tell me the ending and signed the document, the novel is mine and you are a nonentity to me." She cranked out a creepy laugh. "Truthfully, Slayter, when you were dictating your chapters to me and my tape recorder, it was like you were reading a published novel out loud. You could have written every word yourself, then hired a competent editor to fine-tune it. You may have the gift, but not the will to do it yourself. Oh, well. My gain, your loss."

Paige handed him a pen and opened the folder. Slayter looked at his watch again. He still felt okay, but how much longer would Dr. Sinn's temporary antidote last? He had to get the antidote that Sinn gave to Paige into his system as fast as possible. He scanned the page quickly, printed his name on the top line, signed and dated it at the bottom, and closed the manila folder.

"I've fulfilled my part of our deal." He pointed at the capsules on the table. "Which one is Dr. Sinn's antidote? How can you tell the difference?"

"That will remain my secret until you give me the ending."

Slayter studied all the capsules on the table. He was unable to see what was inside, yet Paige had asked him to unveil the ending to his story that she coveted just as much as he desired the antidote. In essence, he would be bartering his story for his life.

"Tell me the ending, Slayter. Which road did Hunter take? Whether you realize it or not, your protagonist, Hunter, is an intriguing character. I love the way you gave him the ability to envision the future after he was knocked unconscious playing college football. He honed his unique gift, only to learn it could also be a curse. So he unselfishly used it to help others until that day he found himself at the crossroads of his life. Which direction did Hunter choose?"

"Hunter combined the three directions into one to become a successful businessman, popular politician, and marry the woman of his dreams to live a perfect life."

"That's brilliant. Hunter is getting what he deserves. And why not? What did helping all those other people get him? Not a damn thing. What do I achieve by editing an author's work? A crummy fee and no notoriety. Hunter wised up and used his gift for himself."

"Which capsule is the antidote," Slayter said in a firm voice.

"It's the one with a tiny blue dot on it." Paige sifted through the capsules with a bright red manicured fingernail until she found the right one. She placed the capsule in her palm and held it out for him to observe. "I put the dot on it to be sure."

Slayter observed the blue dot on the capsule. He reached for it, but her fingers formed into a fist enveloping the pill. Paige stared at him as if she was undecided. Then one by one, her fingers unfolded until the capsule was exposed. He was careful to pluck the antidote from her as if it was a fragile gem that would lose its value if damaged.

"You are positive this is the antidote Dr. Sinn gave to you?" Slayter studied her eyes for a sign that would tell him otherwise. Something was amiss, but for the life of him, he couldn't figure out what it was. "You're absolutely positive."

"I couldn't be more positive," she said.

Slayter swallowed hard. What other choice did he have? He placed the capsule between his thumb and forefinger, then pushed it into his mouth.

Chapter Twenty-Five (1958 Thanksgiving Eve)

Holy placed a hand over his glass to signal Brandi he was more interested in what happened to Slayter Jones than ordering another Scotch and soda. Brandi's head dipped to acknowledge his message, then she turned to Elizabeth.

"Miss Harper," Brandi said, "the hostess asked me to tell you that your fiancé is on his way. While I'm here, is there anything I can get you from the bar?

"Thank you for the message." Elizabeth copied Holy's hand gesture over her glass. The two sherries were still buzzing through her veins. "And no thanks to another drink."

Brandi looked younger than Elizabeth and wore a wedding ring. It sounded weird for the drink runner to refer to her as Miss Harper as if she was closing in on spinsterhood. Elizabeth watched the waitress venture across the room effortlessly carrying a tray loaded with customer's drinks. She glanced at her wristwatch. The time had zipped by. It didn't seem like she had been at Mr. B's for over an hour recounting to Holy what happened in Bobsville three years before. She had never told anyone about that Thanksgiving Day. Maybe the alcohol triggered a need to release what had been building up inside of her. The story's ending would possibly haunt Elizabeth for the rest of her life. Yet by unveiling the events in words, she found it to be therapeutic.

"I'm glad you talked me into staying," Elizabeth said. "I'm still perplexed about why my fiancé asked me to meet him here tonight. Or what he was doing in Oakland on his day off. Then again, if he hadn't asked me, I never would have met a gentleman who has a last name that goes very well with his first name of Holy."

"From a different perspective, I would be alone instead of enjoying the presence of a charming young lady." Holy cracked a sweet smile. "I'm eager to know about the capsule Paige gave to Slayter, but it bothers me to see the hurt in your eyes. I can tell how difficult it is to talk about what happened. Slayter wasn't the only one riding an emotional rollercoaster. Clearly, you were crushed when you learned he had lied, thus blurring your vision of a man you thought would be your partner for the rest of your life."

Holy twisted his wedding band. He stared at the seat across from him, off in a world of his own. Most likely he was thinking about his late wife Margaret and still reeling from the aftermath of a tragedy he would never get over. In a sense, they were sympathizing with each other's heartbreak. He blinked several times and turned to Elizabeth.

"I'm sorry about that," Holy said. "I kind of lost my focus. You'll get old someday, Elizabeth – I pray. Where was I? Oh yes, then you realized Slayter was every bit the man you fell in love with – and more. Plus, you learned he felt the same way about you. My goodness, you went from the lowest of lows to the highest of highs in a matter of minutes. Have you ever wondered what would have happened if Slayter hadn't returned to Warren's house to retrieve his wallet with the dedication of his novel inside?"

"I have pondered that question too many times to count, Holy, and don't have an answer. I was impressed by a man who not only was fighting for his life, he was fighting for the woman he loved. Dr. Sinn made all of us vow not to tell Slayter the ingredients he ingested were nontoxic – for his own good. Then I felt sorry for Slayter when we were on the porch and tried to tell him the truth, but he wouldn't listen to me." Elizabeth gaped into her empty sherry glass. "Our plan for him to go chasing around Bobsville alone to find the antidote was working. After Slayter ran off in the rain to see Paige, I rationalized that telling him the truth about the poison would have been wrong on my part since the whole point of the exercise was to teach him to be dependent on himself and no one else. If I revealed he was never in any real danger of dying, I would have been hurting him, not helping. It also made me realize that enabling someone is a two-way street."

"At that juncture, Elizabeth, you were trying to do the right thing for Slayter by applying some hard discipline for a better purpose. However, if I had been in Slayter's situation, I doubt I would have accepted being told I wasn't in danger. Moreover, even if it had come from Betsy, the young lady I was in love with, I still would have pursued the antidote."

"Perhaps that was also what Slayter was thinking. For the first time, it seemed like he understood how harmful it was for everyone to enable him. In spite of Paige's damaging lie, he was determined to change his ways by following Dr. Sinn's instructions about not allowing help from anyone."

She folded her hands on her lap. It was a well-intentioned plan that turned into a disaster. If only she could have had the ability to see into the future like the character in Slayter's novel. *What If?* was a work of fiction. What happened in real life was hauntingly real.

"Speaking of Paige," Holy said, "she was unrelenting about being the co-author of Slayter's novel. I fully understand Slayter's reluctance to partner with her or anyone else when it came to a story that had been in his head for such a long time. However, since Paige seemed to have contacts in the literary world, perhaps it would have behooved him to at least consider her co-author request."

"Sorry, Holy, but I totally disagree with you," Elizabeth said in a firm voice. "Why would Slayter want to partner up with a person who blatantly lied to make him look bad to others? Don't you realize how wise Slayter was to give Paige that false ending?"

"I had forgotten about that. Why did Slayter give Paige a different ending from the one he shared with you on the front porch? If Paige had a literary agent interested in his novel, wouldn't Slayter be hurting himself in the long run by not giving her the novel's best ending? Then he would really know if he had the talent to be a published author."

"I believe it was just the opposite. Slayter was protecting himself. Most likely the ending he gave to Paige would get rejected. While Paige loved it, her reaction was a perfect example of why her manuscripts had never been published. What do you think Paige would have done if the agent liked the story, but pooh-poohed how it ended? Slayter must have figured she'd go back to him for a new ending. He had his bargaining chip back."

"A shrewd move on Slayter's part. Maybe he was thinking like Hunter in *What If?*"

"Interesting you should say that. It should come as no surprise to you that I'm an avid reader." Elizabeth removed a book from her purse along with black-framed glasses. "I don't go anywhere without a book. Reading novels has always been a pastime for me ever since childhood. Nancy Drew was, and still is, a favorite of mine. Reading was one of the reasons I became a librarian." She put her glasses and book back into her purse. "To do research for Slayter's novel wasn't a chore - it was sheer joy. The ending Slayter gave to Paige would have been unacceptable not only to an agent or publisher, but to a reader who had a vested interest in the story and ending. Literary professionals strive for author name recognition and their characters to provide a continuity that makes a reader eager to buy their next book. The last thing they want is for a reader to feel cheated. That doesn't mean all endings have to be happy, but they should align with the story and character arc. In *What If?,* Hunter was given a special gift that he used to guide others into a better future. When he was at the crossroads, why would Hunter selfishly change into a different person? It made sense only to Paige."

"Have you ever thought about writing a novel of your own, Elizabeth?"

"Of course. Over seventy-five percent of individuals surveyed believed they could write a novel or nonfiction. Slayter was born with a gift. *What If?* and other stories were inside of him waiting to come out. He made it look easy. Believe me, it's not. For any author to complete a first draft is an accomplishment, whether it gets published or not. Paige learned the craft of writing a novel, but she didn't know how to make a reader turn every page. By the way, Turner was her literary name. Paige's real last name was White – like a blank page in a typewriter."

"Obviously Paige, like many individuals, was blinded by ambition," Holy said. "How far was Paige willing to go? My guess is, she was throwing Slayter a major bluff to attain co-authorship. She knew Slayter had more to lose than she did. On the other hand, if Paige wasn't bluffing, she was in great need of a good psychiatrist and being locked away."

"That basically sums it up. Do you mind if I ask what you do for a living?"

"I'm a CPA with my brother Fred. I would retire, but I don't have Margaret to go home to anymore, so I keep working." He took her hand. "Promise me something, Elizabeth."

"How can I promise you something if I don't know what that something is, Holy?"

"If your fiancé arrives before you finish the story, do you promise to tell me the ending?"

"If there was a Holy Bible on the table, I would put my hand on it. You have my word."

"Great." He rubbed his hands together. "What was in the capsule Paige gave to Slayter?"

Chapter Twenty-Six (1955 Thanksgiving Day)

As soon as Slayter popped the capsule into his mouth, he realized what had been bothering him. His tongue defensively sent the capsule back into his fingertips. Something was wrong. Terribly wrong.

He should have realized what Paige was up to as soon as she removed the vial from her purse. Dr. Sinn had said the antidote to the poison he ingested was in powder form. In addition, the doctor had mixed the powder remedy into a liquid that Slayter assumed was water, waited until it settled, and then poured it into a glass.

Slayter placed both hands into his Levi front pockets and produced an emphatic swallow. Paige's eyes lit up as if she had been given a present. The joy in her expression would change if she knew the capsule was tucked deep inside his right pocket.

Sweat formed on Slayter's forehead and neck. He could be sure of only one thing: Paige couldn't be trusted. She had told him the blue dot on the white capsule signified it was the antidote from Dr. Sinn. Yet, there was a good possibility the mark could be an indicator of the exact opposite. If contents inside the capsule were toxic, would the outer cover also be lethal? Tightness spread across his chest. How soon would he know if he reacted too late in removing the capsule from his mouth?

Slayter lifted another capsule from the table and turned it over until a blue dot appeared. Holy venom, the entire antidote scenario was a sham, including Paige sifting through the capsules to find the right one. All the capsules on the table must be tainted. She wasn't taking any chances. Did she somehow insert Dr. Sinn's poison from the Brussels sprouts into the capsules? Or did she put a different kind of poison inside? His eyes questioned her. She, in turn, studied his face, perhaps waiting for him to show more effects from whatever was inside the capsule. They were communicating volumes without saying a word. A line of sweat sneaked into his eye, making it sting. He panted out breaths. Were his nerves running amok? Or was he experiencing symptoms from the poison?

Paige snatched the capsule from his hand, scooped up the other pills off the table and dropped them into the vial. The container went back into her purse. She opened the folder and ran a finger across his printed name, signature, and the date. Satisfied he hadn't tricked her, Paige folded the cover over the paper and placed her purse on top of the folder as if to safeguard it.

Slayter tried to rub the sting from his eye. Paige had said he was a nonentity. Was that due to the admission he just signed? Or was he no longer significant after consuming a white capsule with a blue dot?

"Am I correct in assuming Dr. Sinn never gave you the antidote?" Slayter said.

"Yes, Slayter, but it wouldn't have mattered if Sinn had given it to me. You never would have gotten the antidote." Paige used two fingers on both hands to make quotation marks. "Do you want to know a dirty little secret?" She didn't wait for him to respond. "The portions we put in your Brussels sprouts weren't toxic. It was only a concoction of various foods and spices Sinn whipped up for you to experience those awful symptoms."

Slayter studied her purse as if he had X-ray vision. Could he believe Paige about Dr. Sinn's potion not being toxic? Could he believe anything that came out of Paige's mouth?

"When did you decide to bring Dr. Sinn into the picture?"

"After my roommate, Sally, told me about her crazy great-uncle, Dr. Sinn. I contacted the doctor and told him how you toyed with my affections until I gave in to you. He was very sympathetic and wanted to hear from the other women you abused. Isn't it amazing how a little lie can produce other false accusations? Once Sinn heard from Rhoda, Betsy, and that dolt Doody, he was sold on punishing you."

Slayter wiped his wet forehead with the back of his hand. His heart was pounding. Dr. Sinn led everyone to believe one member of the poison posse was given the antidote. Now it all made sense. He had been chasing after a cure that Dr. Sinn had actually given to him in the lab before he left: the blue-green powder from the envelope.

The doctor's goal was to open Slayter's eyes to how dependent he was on other people. How he took advantage of everyone, but not in the way the poison posse had led Dr. Sinn to believe. Slayter also now understood a slew of well-chosen words would not have changed his mindset after a lifetime of being enabled. Instead, he had to learn the hard way to fully comprehend how he was capable of providing for himself without the aid from others. The harsh – make that cruel – method of teaching him a lesson would have been a success were it not for Paige. She duped everyone to get the rights to his novel. Yet if it weren't for Paige, he would never know how being enabled by others had hurt him.

Slayter looked at his wrist, then shook his head. He would have had less than a half an hour if he was still hunting for the antidote, but that clock didn't matter anymore. Now he was on a different kind of clock that didn't have a face or hands.

"What did you put inside the capsules?" he asked.

"I've been remiss in providing information, haven't I?" she said. "Thanks for reminding me. That capsule contains some of the most toxic poison in the world when ingested. I learned about it from a former client of mine who was a chemist by trade. He was a genius in the lab, but dreadfully untalented in front of a typewriter. The poison comes from the ovaries and innards of a funny-looking puffy sea creature. The chemist showed me a batch of it in his lab one day, then demonstrated the immediacy of its potency on a lab rat. In less than ten minutes, the chemist was as dead as the rat after I put several drops of it in his coffee. Why fail from leaving a trail? I removed the poison from the lab and have been saving it for just the right time. The effects are respiratory arrest and paralysis. Death can be immediate or within an hour." She grinned like the Cheshire cat in *Alice in Wonderland*. "Thanks for the ending to your novel. You really have talent, Slayter. P. T. Barnum was right about a sucker born every minute."

Slayter had trouble swallowing. By her telling him about a murder she committed and another she was about to commit, Paige assumed he would be dead soon. It was just a matter of when. His book dedication to Betsy may never see a publisher's ink.

"How do you expect to explain my dead body?" He struggled for air.

"No problem. Old Dr. Sinn got his chemicals mixed up. Betsy, Rhoda, Doody, and the doctor will pay the consequences, along with a talented author named Slayter Jones."

Slayter darted into the kitchen. He picked up the black phone's receiver to dial Betsy's number. He stopped after two numbers. There was no dial tone; the line was dead, most likely from the storm.

"You should have said something, Slayter," Paige said. "I would have told you to save what little energy you have left. The phone has been out for over an hour. I would imagine the more you exert yourself, the faster you will die."

Slayter brushed Paige with his shoulder as he filed out of the kitchen and back to the dinette table. Her purse was heavier than expected when he threw it across the living room, knocking over a table lamp. Paige gasped, looking frightened for the first time. She ran for her purse as Slayter dashed out of the apartment with the folder in hand.

He took the stairs two at a time, sliding his hand on the rail to avoid falling. He burst through the first-floor door and almost ran over two elderly ladies on their way to the elevator. Once outside, he could still hear their flustered responses. He sprinted into the moist night. The rain was refreshing. How much stamina did he have left? He rounded a corner and splashed up water from a puddle. Doody's truck remained double parked behind the Bug. The cab light showed Doody smoking a cigarette and reading *Lolita.* Slayter slammed his palm against the passenger window, causing Doody to drop his cigarette onto the page. Lolita was smoking hot in more ways than one.

Slayter opened the passenger door, releasing a wave of smoke. Grumbling, Doody stubbed out the cigarette in the ashtray. Slayter lifted the walkie-talkie from the seat.

"Dr. Sinn," Slayter shouted into the radio. "Come in, Dr. Sinn. This is Slayter. *Over.* "

"Why are you on the radio, Mr. Jones? Where's Larry? What did you do to him? *Over.*"

"Doody's fine, Dr. Sinn. I now know you gave me the true antidote in your lab. The one thing you didn't count on when you were trying to teach me to fend for myself was to have one of your poison partners go rogue." Slayter paused to catch his breath. "Paige lied about me and it snowballed into other lies. She may have poisoned me for real. I should know in a couple more minutes. *Over.*"

"You are asking me to trust you over what everyone else has told me about you? Put Larry on to corroborate your story. *Over.*"

"Doody can't help you. I got my information the hard way from each poisoner. *Over.*"

"Surely, you don't expect me to believe you without hearing from the others. *Over.*"

Slayter's first inclination was go grab Doody's shirt and shake some sense into him – a useless task. Instead, he put the radio into Doody's hand and urged him with his eyes.

"This is Larry, Dr. Sinn. I don't know anything, but I believe Slayter is tellin' the truth."

"Why would I be calling you if I'm aware you didn't really poison me?" Slayter said, after grabbing the radio back. "Paige is bonkers. You're in grave danger, along with Betsy, Rhoda, and Doody. Do you have anything in the office to protect yourself? *Over.*"

Doody's eyes grew large. He threw *Lolita* onto the dashboard and reached for another cigarette while the one in the ashtray was smoldering.

"This is all very confusing, Mr. Jones. Why would Paige want to harm any of us? *Over.*"

"Ultimately, if I die from the poison she gave to me, you and the others are going to be held responsible for my death. However, I have a feeling Paige wants everyone involved out of the way – meaning dead – so there is no trail leading back to her. *Over.*"

"You said Paige poisoned you. How and with what? And why? *Over.*"

"Paige wants ownership of my novel that she has been editing. She gave me a capsule and said it was your antidote. As soon as I put it in my mouth, I remembered you saying the antidote was in powder form. I removed the capsule as quickly as I could without her knowing it. Since Paige is under the impression I swallowed the capsule, she told me it was loaded with some kind of poisonous fish guts. *Over.*"

"There are many sea creatures that produce toxic poisons. Your quick thinking may have saved you. Come back to my office so I can assist you medically if needed. *Over.*"

"I don't have time, Dr. Sinn. The phone lines are down and I need to warn Betsy. I'm going to send Doody to alert Rhoda. It might be wise if we all meet at your office. *Over.*"

"Of course." Dr. Sinn heaved a breath into the radio. "My sincere apologies, Mr. Jones, for misjudging you. Nothing like this has ever happened before. *Over.*"

Slayter tossed the walkie-talkie back onto the seat. Doody made no attempt to pick it up.

"I don't get it," Doody said. "Why would Paige want to hurt me? Or anyone else? Are you sure you ain't sayin' all of this to shove the blame away from yourself?"

"I'll explain it to you later – if there is a later. You need to hurry to Warren's house and warn Rhoda about Paige. Then go to the police department and tell them everything you heard me say to Dr. Sinn. The police need to go to Dr. Sinn's office as quickly as possible. Don't stop for anyone or anything. Just tear ass straight outta here, Doody."

Slayter jumped back before Doody ran over his toes when the truck peeled out. Back in the Bug, he opened the drenched folder. The rain had smudged his printed name and signature making it unreadable. The document was worthless. He flipped the folder onto the floorboard and jammed down on the accelerator until first gear whined mercy back at him. He shifted and turned in the opposite direction of the parking lot exit. The Bug skidded to a stop in front of Paige's parking space. It was vacant. Damn.

Slayter left the apartment complex without stopping to see if any traffic was coming from either direction. He wasn't feeling any additional weird effects from the capsule that had been in his mouth. Maybe he dodged Paige's attempt to poison him, but another dilemma was heading his way. The gas needle was leaning toward empty again. It might come down to what would conk out first: him or the Bug.

Betsy's house was less than five minutes away. Where would Paige go first? How could he outwit her demented, cunning mind?

There was a big difference between dealing with Doody's unpredictable brain versus guessing what Paige would do. Slayter's only advantage was that Paige thought he had ingested the poisonous capsule and would have as little as ten minutes and no more than an hour to live. Logically, Paige would assume he would go to the only person who could save him, Dr. Sinn. Slayter pressed harder on the gas pedal. With Paige's head start, he prayed his logic was right.

Slayter zoomed through a dip in the road, splashing waves of water like a motorboat. If the Harpers had any doubt about his sanity, they were going to think he had gone bananas with his story about Paige. Better to have them think he was nutso than to be unaware of Paige's intentions. Once Slayter informed the Harpers, Betsy would be well protected by Mr. Harper's rifle and Grandma Harper's frying pan.

He didn't slow down for a stop sign. A horn blast to his left caught his attention. A car was careening towards him. He sent the gas pedal to the floor and squeezed the steering wheel expecting a collision in the intersection. The other car went into a sideways skid and nicked the Bug's back bumper. Slayter managed to keep the front end on course and yelled apologies the other driver would never hear. Two more blocks to Betsy's house. If adrenaline was keeping him alive, he hoped there was another minute's worth.

Slayter's tense shoulders relaxed after he turned onto the Harpers' street.

"What the hell..." He laid on the steering wheel horn and didn't let up. "No!"

Betsy slid onto the front passenger seat of Paige's red Plymouth and closed the door.

Paige sped away from the Harper house. Why would Betsy go anywhere with Paige?

Chapter Twenty-Seven (1955 Thanksgiving Day)

Slayter forced his little car to maximum speed, but he was losing ground to Paige's Plymouth Belvedere at an alarming rate. When it came to horsepower, it was like a pony chasing a thoroughbred. He pushed hard on the steering wheel horn and didn't let up, but Paige wouldn't slow down.

If Slayter knew where Paige was going, he might have an opportunity to stop her. Just as important, he needed to find out why Betsy was riding shotgun in Paige's car – two women who couldn't be more opposite. When he told Paige about Betsy's involvement with his novel, Paige must have gone psycho. Betsy was now aware Paige's lie started the poison process in motion. He shivered after thinking the unthinkable. A Betsy-Paige connection didn't make sense, unless Betsy was in cahoots with Paige? Had they been tricking him the whole time? If so, it was a hundred times worse than having them play a malicious ruse on him. After Betsy tearfully professed her love for him, was she acting? Playing a part to shield her role in a scheme to steal his novel? If Betsy was involved with Paige, her impressive performance was worthy of an Oscar.

He couldn't believe what he was considering. As illogical as a liaison between Paige and Betsy sounded, it was possible. Before today, he never would have thought people close to him would taint his food to produce excruciating pain and discomfort or push him into ingesting poison inside a capsule. His head shot back after another startling thought took possession of his mind. The circumstances had produced an ironic switcheroo. Betsy was made to believe he lied to her and now he was considering something similar about Betsy. Paige had lost control of her sanity. Perhaps he was doing the same thing.

"Betsy would never betray me," he shouted, squeezing the gearshift knob and scolding himself for doubting Betsy's loyalty. "There has to be another reason why she's riding in Paige's car.

Whether Betsy knew it or not, she has put herself in great danger."

Up ahead, Paige's red car disappeared from view after turning left at a corner without braking. Slayter stopped honking. Most likely Paige was heading to Dr. Sinn's office. If not there, she could be on her way to see Rhoda. Hopefully Doody was able to warn Slayter's sister-in-law and brother. Slayter's gut told him to go with his first instinct. How could he get to Dr. Sinn's office before Paige? Following her wasn't an option. However, he had grown up in Bobsville and knew every shortcut in town. He could bypass several blocks by taking back roads and cutting through alleys. Was that enough to put him ahead of her? Or he could roll the dice and take a cross-country motorcycle path known as Daredevil's Delight that would put him a few minutes from Dr. Sinn's office. Or it could also get him stuck in a muddy rut and useless to all except Percy the Pig and other critters. Taking Daredevil's Delight was more of a reckless gamble than a practical way to solve his dilemma.

His gas gauge made the decision for him. The needle was on empty. He'd take the route that had the shortest distance to Dr. Sinn, his best chance of not running out of gas.

The Bug blasted past the block where Paige had made her turn. The race was on, but not just to beat Paige to Dr. Sinn's office. By now, Doody should have alerted Warren and Rhoda about Paige and be on his way to the Bobsville Police Station. Slayter's throat tightened. Was Doody capable of repeating to the police what Slayter had said to Dr. Sinn over the walkie-talkie? Would the police even believe Doody? Slayter was having trouble swallowing. If Doody had come to him with the same convoluted story, would he accept what Doody was telling him as true? Slayter hacked out a dry cough. He may have made a huge mistake by sending Doody to the police, but what other choice did he have? Plus, it was too late now.

Slayter had two more blocks before he would have to make a turn that would lead him to the Daredevil's Delight path. So far, he wasn't experiencing symptoms from the poison capsule. A good sign, but if the effects from the poison suddenly struck him down, how many days would it take to discover his dead body inside the Bug? It was imperative that he traverse the path as quickly as possible.

The rain had stopped. Another good sign. He turned onto the street that led to the path. The dirt was as hard as cement in the summer and dangerous in the winter. His eyes continued to look back and forth between the road and gas gauge until the pavement turned into mud. The bug started to skid and slide. He ceased looking at the gauge and concentrated on the road as his hands tightened on the steering wheel to keep control.

His headlights picked up a narrow opening to a path guarded by wood posts on each side. The entrance was designed to keep normal sized vehicles from fitting through the entryway. Slayter knew from experience the Bug could get by with an inch on each side to spare. He slowed his speed, took a deep breath, and squeezed through the posts without difficulty. The only illumination came from his headlights as he entered a sea of darkness. He was comfortable driving on the path in the daylight, but it was difficult to navigate in the dark.

Slayter's foot kept jumping on and off the accelerator. He had to drive fast enough not to get bogged down in the mud and slow enough to handle his car. His eyes squeezed together like he was staring into a bright sun. He didn't dare shift his view from the road to the speedometer. So far, the tires were holding their traction in the muck.

His butt hurt from bouncing on the hard bucket. He was holding the steering wheel so tight his fingers cramped. If he lessened his grip, he might lose control. It took all of his discipline not to peek at the gas gauge. Movement to his left made him hit the brake pedal. Something was running alongside the Bug as if they were racing. A deer. Under normal circumstances he would have accepted the challenge, but nothing was normal about driving on this muddy trail in the dark. He hit the horn to protect Bambi and his Bug from damaging each other. The doe veered away.

If anything, the night became murkier. It felt like he was in a dark tunnel with no end in sight. The road bent to the left, giving him his bearings. He was entering Dead Man's Curve. Was every major curve in a road labeled Dead Man's Curve? Or did some doofus motorcyclist kill himself on it? He notched down his speed. He had traveled over half of the way. It seemed like he had been driving for hours. The cramping in his fingers on the steering wheel had traveled to his forearms. He removed one hand from the steering wheel and shook some life into it. Then he repeated the same exercise with the other hand. His head pounded from the intense concentration of dealing with the conditions.

The moment he survived the curve, heavy raindrops began to bomb the area. As hard as they tried, the windshield wipers couldn't keep up with the downpour. His visibility was greatly limited. Slayter's desire to get to the end of the trail quickly was being tested. He downshifted and eased off the gas pedal. Wind currents as well as bad traction made it seem like he was no longer on ground. The Bug swerved from one side to the other. He wasn't in danger of falling off a cliff, but he was close to swerving off the path into a downhill slide. Once the tires left the trail, the Bug would skid down a hill of wet weeds and brush into the unknown with no chance of ever getting back onto the path again.

Slayter wrestled the steering wheel to force the Bug back into the middle of the road. At least he wouldn't have to worry about hitting another vehicle. What other damn fool would be crazy enough to travel Daredevil's Delight on a stormy night?

Slayter pushed harder on the gas once he entered a straightaway. How much time had he wasted by decreasing his speed over and over again? In hindsight, by taking this route he may have blown every chance he had at beating Paige to Dr. Sinn's office. For some inane reason the roles the people involved in teaching him a lesson had been reversed. They were now dependent on him, except for Paige. He peeked at the gas gauge. The needle had moved to the left of center on the E. He was close to the end of the trail. Close wouldn't work until he was off the mud and onto a paved street.

"Come on, baby. Hang in there." Slayter patted the dash as if it was a faithful canine like Stubby. He'd never talked to his car before. If there ever was a time he needed someone or something to enable him, it was now. "All I need is a couple of minutes more."

The front end crashed down after hitting a dip in the trail, splashing water up over the hood and windshield on both sides. The paint canister tipped, throwing him off balance. Both feet left the pedal area so he could right himself. The Bug slowed, making the engine lug its displeasure. His feet reengaged to their respective pedals to pick up the momentum before he would become mired in the mud. The windshield wipers cleared some of the muck from the glass. To his amazement and delight, he could see blurry lights in the background. He was close to the end of his cross-country trek.

Slayter pushed the accelerator too hard and almost squirmed off the path. His foot backed off until he was at a speed that worked better. The Bug squeezed through the posts without doing more damage to its body and hit the pavement like a racecar. In less than a minute, Slayter entered Bobsville's industrial area and sped past Thingamabobs Inc., the only major factory in town. The next block consisted of several small warehouses and a hodgepodge of small businesses. He took a right turn, then a quick left into an alley – a shortcut that would save him time. With no traffic to contend with, he bombed down the alley. For the second time this Thanksgiving, his Bug ran out of gas.

Slayter jumped out of his car after coasting to a stop. He didn't bother to lock the door. After the beating the bug had taken tonight, it would get voted most ugly on a used car lot. He ran into wind and rain, grateful he had gotten this far. He was soaked by the time he made it out of the alley and into a section of neighborhood housing. He didn't have to contend with any cars or foot traffic. Nothing was moving except for him. Dr. Sinn's office was only a few minutes away by foot. A stitch of pain that runners often felt jabbed his stomach. He hoped the hurt would go away as suddenly as it came.

But the pain in his stomach was getting worse. Maybe it wasn't from running. Maybe it came from the poison capsule. One more block and he could stop. He rounded a corner and sprinted down the sidewalk to Dr. Sinn's office. His vision was blurred due to the rain mixed with sweat. He couldn't tell if Paige's car was parked on the street or not. The pain eased, but he was losing his wind. With what little breath he had left, Slayter willed himself to keep pumping his legs.

Slayter plopped down on the walkway leading to the entrance of Dr. Sinn's office. He gasped for air. Paige's car was nowhere to be found. He struggled to his feet, still trying to catch his breath. Did he beat Paige to Dr. Sinn's office? Or had he guessed wrong about where Paige would go? If it was the latter, how could he help Betsy?

A gunshot rang out from inside the doctor's office sending Slayter scrambling to the front door.

Chapter Twenty-Eight (1955 Thanksgiving Day)

Slayter raced into the doctor's office and zipped through an empty waiting room. The examination room was also vacant. He found Dr. Sinn in his lab with his back turned to the doorway. The room reeked of sulfur from gun powder. The doctor twisted around and pointed a long-barreled pistol at Slayter after he entered the room.

Slayter ceded by raising his arms high in the air. The gun looked like it had come straight from the shooting hand of Wild West hombre Wyatt Earp. Had everyone gone batcrap crazy? Where was Marshal Matt Dillon when he needed him?

Dr. Sinn lowered his hand and placed the pistol on the counter. He turned his head to the left and gazed at the bullet hole in the wall above the shelf that featured a jar containing a tiny defenseless creature floating in lime-green liquid with his little arms raised. Why would Dr. Sinn fire a shot into the office wall?

"Sorry if I frightened you, Mr. Jones," Dr. Sinn said. "I was scared out of my wits after you warned me about Paige. I figured it would be a good idea to give the pretense of my being armed just in case she did show up – the gun being a prop, if you will."

"A prop that fires real bullets," Slayter said, lowering his arms.

"I've never fired a gun before in my life." Dr. Sinn nudged the pistol further away from him with a finger. His breathing was labored. "I figured it wasn't loaded. Not only was it full of bullets, the darn thing also has a hair trigger."

"Why would you own a real gun, especially if you had no use for it?

"In the thirties, right in the middle of the Great Depression, I treated a patient who didn't have any money to pay my fee. Instead, he gave me his only possession that had value – his granddaddy's gun. Bartering was more prevalent in those days. I told him it wasn't necessary to pay me, but he insisted I take the pistol." Dr. Sinn paused to scowl at the weapon. "Menacing piece of metal, isn't it? I think

I kept the gun around if the patient ever wanted it back – kind of like a pawn shop. Once again, Mr. Jones, you have my deepest apologies. I made a dreadful mistake. As I told you over the walkie-talkie radio, nothing like this has ever happened to me before. Obviously, it's time for me to take down my doctor's shingle and find another hobby."

"Unfortunately, Dr. Sinn, your retirement is one lesson too late," Slayter said. "Look, I get it. Believe it or not, I'm grateful you opened my eyes about my being reliant solely on others." He placed a hand on his stomach. "I'm just not too keen about your method. You indicated to me earlier that you have been providing this service successfully for a long time. I find it amazing no one has ever taken you to task. Or something unanticipated has backfired on you. In my case, that unexpected thing was Paige."

"In all candor," Dr. Sinn uttered in a weak voice, "I now realize how blinded I was by my previous success. I expected a positive outcome for each lesson. In the end, I guess every venture has potential downfalls." He placed both palms on the counter to steady himself. "You said Paige may have poisoned you. Are you feeling any effects from the capsule you put in your mouth?"

"So far, nothing unordinary." Slayter held up crossed fingers. "I may have lucked out."

"Do you have any idea where Paige is now?"

"No clue as to her whereabouts," Slayter said. "I tried to follow her, but she had a head start and a faster car. I was convinced she'd come after you or Betsy first before doing away with everyone else involved in the scheme. The last time I saw Paige, Betsy was in her car heading your way. Before you ask, I'm still baffled why Betsy would be with Paige, but I fear for Betsy's safety. Maybe Paige went to my brother's house first. Doody was supposed to warn Rhoda and Warren and then alert the police to come here. Have you communicated with Doody on the walkie-talkie?"

"No," Dr. Sinn said. "I called him several times with no response."

"With Doody, there's no telling what that means." Slayter looked down at the floor and shook his head.

"I'm still in the fog about Paige's reason to poison you. Did you perhaps give her a false impression that she was hired to be more than an editor and you reneged on the deal?"

"My author/editor relationship with Paige was a bit unusual, but I never told Paige or put in writing that she could be a co-author or author of my story." Slayter pointed both forefingers at the doctor. "Hey, you made me realize how naïve I've been to allow people do things for me. I didn't even realize that creating a novel meant I had to actually go through the process of writing it, as silly as that may sound. Instead, I dictated my story to her into a tape recorder. She transcribed my words and typed them in a novel format, chapter by chapter, except for the last chapter. Just so you understand, Dr. Sinn, Paige wasn't my ghostwriter. She was my ghost-recorder. That was our agreement."

"That still doesn't explain why..."

Dr. Sinn wiped his forehead. His eyelids fluttered like he might pass out. He winced as if he was in pain.

"Dr. Sinn, are you all right?" Slayter asked.

"It'll pass, Mr. Jones. Please continue so I can better comprehend why Paige went off the deep end."

"Earlier tonight, I learned Paige was unsuccessful in getting her own writing published. Unbeknownst to me, she sent several of my novel chapters – under her name, not mine – to an agent who then wanted to see the entire manuscript. The agent's interest must have sparked something in Paige that she couldn't control. Maybe she thought it would be her only chance to get published and she deserved the honor more than I did. What I do know for a fact, Paige concocted a complete falsehood that prompted the other people involved to lie, all at my expense. She fooled everyone, including you Dr. Sinn, to go against me."

"Oh, my," Dr. Sinn moaned, placing a hand on his chest. "What have I done? But why would Paige want to harm Rhoda, Betsy, Larry, and...me?"

"If you count my brother Warren, each individual you named knew I was working with editor Paige Turner, although Betsy was the only other person who had read all of the paper chapters Paige produced from the recordings. In fact, now that I recall, it was Paige's name, not mine, on all of the page headers. Think about it, Dr. Sinn. If Paige eliminated all of us, the novel would be hers and no one would know the difference. All she needed was my last chapter. Paige told me you gave her the antidote. She wouldn't hand it over unless I divulged how my story ended. The antidote was *barter* for my last chapter since I didn't know you had already given me the antidote in your office."

Dr. Sinn winced in pain. If possible, his skin was more ashen than before. Heavy breaths panted from his mouth as if he couldn't breathe through his nose. His body wobbled down onto an unsteady three-legged stool. He removed his glasses and rubbed his eyes. The bravado he had demonstrated from their first visit had taken a 180-degree turn. The more Dr. Sinn was digesting Paige's motive and how she had set him up, the heavier the burden weighed on him. Maybe, in hindsight, Dr. Sinn was trying to figure out how he could have seen through Paige's act and refused to play a role in her scheme? Or did he finally come to the realization his last mission was a perfect springboard for an obsessed and crazy woman to change her status in the literary world by teaching him a cruel lesson he'd never forget?

Slayter moved to end of the counter and lifted the phone receiver to his ear. There was no dial tone – the lines were still down. Slayter replaced the receiver back to its base and moved around the counter to Dr. Sinn's side. Looking down at the doctor, Slayter recalled what Dr. Sinn had said to him while he was suffering under the influence of the doctor's potion: "Mr. Jones, you don't look so hot either."

"Dr. Sinn, is your car here?" Slayter asked.

"What…my car. Yes. It's parked at the curb in front of the office. Why do you ask?"

"I'm not trying to play doctor here, doc, but you need medical attention. The phone lines are still down. I'll drive you to Dr. Tyme's house."

Slayter watched the doctor squirm in pain. Once he put Dr. Sinn in Dr. Tyme's care, he could try to track down Paige and Betsy in Dr. Sinn's car.

"Why on earth would you help me after what I did to you, Mr. Jones?"

"You need assistance, and I'm the only person who can make that happen. Where are your car keys?"

"I don't need Tyme to diagnose my condition." Dr. Sinn's eyes watered. "It's my heart. There's no need to take me anywhere. Get my pills. They're in the desk in my office which is the room adjacent to the examination room – top drawer on the right. My heart pills are the only vial in that drawer, so you can't miss them. No need for water. I just let the pill dissolve under my tongue. If you don't mind, please hurry."

Slayter hustled to the office. On top of the desk was another framed photo of the young woman who broke Goodwin Axel Sinn's heart. The vial was exactly where Dr. Sinn said it would be. Slayter removed the container from the drawer, not knowing for sure how many pills the doctor would need and ran back to the lab.

"You were wise to bring the vial," Dr. Sinn said. "At times, when I don't get immediate results, I take an additional pill."

Slayter removed the lid and poured one white tablet into Dr. Sinn's hand. The doctor placed it under his tongue and closed his eyes. Slayter stood next to him waiting for a response. He was silently rooting for the doctor, not knowing what else he could do.

Dr. Sinn's eyelids popped open. "Another, Mr. Jones. One more tablet, please."

Slayter hesitated. If he gave Dr. Sinn another pill, would it cure him or kill him? The doctor's trembling hand was urging Slayter for his antidote. Slayter dropped one more pill into Dr. Sinn's palm. This time, it didn't take long for the medicine to take effect. Dr. Sinn opened his eyes and sucked in air as fast as he could. His torso seemed to relax. He nodded to Slayter with a tight smile.

"Thank you, Mr. Jones. You saved me. I doubt I could've made it to my desk. Truth be known, I've been living on borrowed time for quite a while."

"What else can I do for you, doc?" Slayter asked.

"I'll be okay for the time being. Take my Desoto and find Paige before she hurts Betsy or anyone else. My keys are in my suit pocket hanging on the coat rack in my office."

"I'd feel better if I could take you to Dr. Tyme's house, then do what I have to do to find Betsy—"

"Slayter! Slayter!" Betsy shouted from the lobby. She ran into the lab and flew into Slayter's arms. If they were on a football field, Betsy would have been flagged for unnecessary roughness, not that he minded.

"What a touching scene," Paige said, standing in the doorway swinging her purse.

Chapter Twenty-Nine (1955 Thanksgiving Day)

As much as Slayter was enjoying Betsy's embrace, he couldn't take his eyes off of Paige. She worked her way into the lab and claimed squatter's rights after placing her purse on a table in the corner next to a microscope. The same heavy purse Slayter had chucked across the living room floor before fleeing from her apartment. Why did Paige bring Betsy to Dr. Sinn's office?

"Good lord, Slayter, you're soaking wet." Betsy kissed Slayter's cheek, backed away, and examined him from head to toe as if she was the doctor. "I was so worried about you. Paige told me you were being treated by Dr. Sinn for some kind of injury. Did your stomach pain return? Were you wounded? Please tell me what is wrong with you."

Slayter pulled at his wet shirt sticking to his chest. He was relieved Betsy was safe, and now he knew why she was in Paige's car. Paige had conned Betsy into believing he had been hurt, knowing exactly how Betsy would respond. More than ever, he needed to be on guard and figure out what Paige was up to before she struck.

Paige was still wearing the same astonished expression she exhibited while standing in the doorway; the kind of look a person would have when they believed they were seeing a ghost. He didn't need extrasensory perception to know what she was thinking: why is Slayter Jones here and still alive after ingesting a capsule full of poison?

"Dr. Sinn," Betsy said, in an exasperated tone, "Slayter isn't saying what you treated him for. I want to help if I can. Would you please tell me what is wrong with Slayter?"

Dr. Sinn removed his glasses. His head shook in confusion.

"Slow down, Betsy. There's nothing wrong with me." Slayter held her by the shoulders as he answered for the doctor. "Paige lied to you. Again. I saw you get into Paige's car. I tried to follow her but couldn't keep up. Didn't you hear me honking my horn after she drove off? And what took you so long to get here?"

"I'd like to answer those questions, if I may?" Paige didn't wait for permission. "We didn't hear your horn because it was raining hard and I had the radio on for weather updates. I don't have to tell you how nasty it is out there. Twice we had to turn around and find an alternate route to Dr. Sinn's office because of fallen trees or branches blocking the road. We were fortunate that we made it here at all."

Paige's gray eyes illuminated as she smiled at Slayter, then at Dr. Sinn. A look that could persuade a grand jury she was more pure and innocent than Mother Teresa. A look that made him believe she would act in good faith as a hired literary editor for his novel. And a look that could easily convince an empathetic person like Betsy to believe any story she invented as authentic. The other poison posse members had never seen the flip side of Paige, where her warm eyes turned icy cold while friendly lips sneered tight.

"Why is there a gun on the counter, Dr. Sinn?" Paige pointed at the long-barreled pistol. "Is it for your protection? Or did Slayter threaten you like he threatened me? I won't repeat the vile things he said he would do to me if I didn't give him the antidote."

"I did feel a need to protect myself, but not from Slayter," the doctor said.

"Slayter, please listen to me." Betsy put her hand on his arm. "You had every right to be angry with Paige because she lied about what you did, or more accurately, didn't do. But I think you have it all wrong about Paige. She told me you were upset when she didn't have the antidote. By the way, Dr. Sinn, *who* did you trust with the antidote?"

"Myself," Dr. Sinn said in a feeble voice. "I gave Mr. Jones the antidote before he left my office, but I told him it was only temporary and he had three hours to contact all of the individuals involved. I was hoping the experience would shock him into understanding he didn't need to be reliant on anyone but himself."

"Paige said she would have given you the antidote if she had it, Slayter," Betsy continued. "She deceived us because she was in love with you and jealous of our relationship. I know that doesn't excuse her bad behavior but being in love can make us do some crazy things. Fortunately, Paige came to her senses and apologized for the trouble she had caused – not just to you, but to everyone. She sincerely wanted to make amends, starting with driving me to see you after she learned you had been injured."

Slayter observed Dr. Sinn's slight head nod in support of Betsy's explanation. Paige couldn't have a better spokeswoman. The temperature in the lab was chilly, but the doctor's flushed cheeks glistened with perspiration. Was it the medication that caused him to sweat so profusely? Or did Betsy sway the doctor into having second thoughts about how Slayter portrayed Paige's evilness? If so, in a matter of minutes, two members of Slayter's team had switched sides. From one extreme to the next. Would his life ever be easy again? Before today, someone would always jump in and fix things for him whether he asked or not. Now, he was on his own flying solo.

"Betsy, if Paige didn't tell you I had been injured and was being treated at Dr. Sinn's office, would you have gone with her?" Slayter asked.

Betsy paused to consider the question. "When you put it that way, Slayter, I definitely would not have believed Paige or agreed to go with her. But I didn't hesitate when she said you were hurt."

"Did Paige happen to tell you how she knew I had been injured?"

"No, she didn't say." Betsy cocked her head to the side, then looked at Paige. "How did you know Slayter had been hurt?"

"From Slayter, of course," Paige said in a calm voice without missing a beat. "He said he was in terrible pain when he showed up at my apartment, but I never did find out what was wrong with him. Perhaps he got hurt in the storm. Or could it be that Slayter couldn't handle what we put him through, even if it was for his own good. Maybe he got paranoid and had a meltdown. But, make no mistake, Betsy, Slayter stayed long enough to show his nasty side after he found out I didn't have the antidote. When he left my apartment empty handed, he looked like a deflated balloon."

Slayter's stomach jumped. Paige may not have the talent to create a publishable novel, but she could write the ultimate book on how to deceive others. Did Paige dupe him about the capsule being filled with poison fish guts? Had she literally told him a big fish story that had nothing to do with bragging and everything to do with a big bluff that would prompt him to yield authorship of his novel?

Dr. Sinn's mouth was fixed open, panting out breaths at an alarming rate. The poor guy was weakening fast. Time was a pressing issue again. Sinn needed to be in Dr. Tyme's care as soon as possible. Slayter couldn't wait any longer for Paige to make her move. Most likely, she coerced Betsy into going to Dr. Sinn's office for one reason: to do away with both of them. Now Paige could add Slayter to her kill menu.

A motion in the hallway caught Slayter's eye. Officer Eddie Rose was standing a foot from the doorway with a finger to his lips. Doody was next to him. Paige couldn't see them from her angle. Slayter removed the capsule from his pocket and displayed it. The casing was sticky from moisture or leakage. Could the poison seep through his skin?

"Here's the real story, Dr. Sinn," Slayter said. "Although Paige rightly denied receiving an antidote from you, she tried to deceive me. She gave me the capsule in my hand as your antidote in return for me giving her sole ownership of the story she transcribed and edited. I faked taking the capsule when I remembered you had said the antidote came in powdered form." He put the pill on the counter and wiped his hand on his jeans. "Paige then informed me that I had consumed a lethal poison and was sure to die."

"I don't know where you got that...*capsule*, Slayter." Paige's eyebrows arched high into her forehead. "But it certainly didn't come from me."

"You continue to be fuzzy on the facts, Paige. Let me refresh your memory. The capsule came from a vial inside your purse. Empty your purse and prove me wrong."

Eddie moved into the lab. Doody tried to follow him, but Eddie pushed a hand out like a traffic cop for Doody to stay in the hallway.

"Officer Rose, ma'am. I would like to see if you have pills like the one Slayter just displayed."

"Officer, I do have a vial of pills in my purse." Paige clutched her bag as if it was loaded with gold bars. "They're prescription. The only way Slayter would have known about my pills is if he stole one when he was in my apartment earlier. Simple as that."

"Give it up, Paige," Slayter said. "You can't win. It's over."

"Would you please show me the pill container in your purse, ma'am," Eddie said.

Slayter stiffened when Paige reached into her purse. She removed the glass vial and shook the contents as if she was ringing a bell.

"I don't see a label on the container to verify the contents are a prescription," Eddie said. "What type of medicine are you taking and for what reason?"

"It's personal and quite frankly none of your business."

"Why is there no label? Would you please empty what is in the vial onto the desk?"

"I peeled off the label," Paige admitted. "To my knowledge that isn't against the law."

"I believe you are correct, ma'am."

"If you must know, they are for female cramps. Would you like to try one, officer?"

"No, ma'am. That would be against the law for me to take another person's prescription."

Betsy snuggled close to Slayter. He put an arm around her and glanced at Dr. Sinn. His eyelids fluttered as if he might faint. For everyone's sake, it was the last five seconds of the game. Paige's intentions needed to be flushed out.

"Since you say those pills are prescribed by a doctor," Slayter said, "why don't you take one to demonstrate to the officer that they aren't poisonous?"

"Belay what Mr. Jones just asked you to do, ma'am. Please show me the capsules."

"I already took one this morning." Paige spilled the capsules out on the table.

"I appreciate your cooperation, ma'am," Officer Rose said. "Just so you know, I radioed the station to provide the information Doody relayed to me. Another squad car is on its way as backup."

Paige focused on Slayter. If a stare could shoot poison darts, he would be dead.

"Back at your apartment, Paige, you were in the mood to negotiate," Slayter said. "I think you were lying to me about poison being in the capsules. I'm so sure you were lying, if you swallow one of those capsules, I'll sign an agreement to transfer the authorship of my novel to you. Isn't that what you wanted? Hey, this time you've got witnesses to verify our agreement is legitimate and one of them is a sworn officer of the law."

"You bastard, Slayter. We could have made a great team." Paige scooped up several capsules, shoved them into her mouth, and choked them down. "I'll show you how smart you are. If I can't have a published book, then you and the librarian won't have one either."

Paige removed a gun from her purse and aimed the barrel at Betsy. Slayter pushed Betsy away as Paige pulled the trigger.

Two booming gunshots rang out simultaneously, before a third shot was fired. Smoke rose toward the ceiling, followed by silence.

Chapter Thirty (1958 Thanksgiving Eve)

The background din in the lounge quieted after Holy bellowed, "What happened?"

Elizabeth could hear the bartender drop ice cubes into a glass following Holy's outburst. Reliving the episode in Dr. Sinn's lab had left her spent. She closed her eyes, feeling a sense of relief for telling her story, something she had never been able to do. Yet, to her dismay, discussing the tragedy didn't remove a stockpile of torment that would most likely haunt her for the rest of her life.

"You can't leave me hanging like that, Elizabeth," Holy said in an urgent tone. "What happened after the gunshots were fired?"

Her eyelids lifted in stages. Did she have enough energy to go on? In all fairness to Holy, whether she wanted to or not, she couldn't hold off answering his question about what occurred next. She took a deep breath, then another, before indicating with a head movement she would finish the story that forever changed her life.

"First and foremost," she said, "I'm fortunate to be alive. I will never forgive myself for being conned by Paige to go with her to Dr. Sinn's office. If that wasn't bad enough, I attempted to convince Slayter that Paige wasn't the monster of a person he knew she was. I was standing side by side with Slayter when Paige pulled the gun from her purse and aimed it at me. Thank God he had the wherewithal to shove me out of harm's way, otherwise I wouldn't be here right now. I was sprawled out on the lab floor when two gunshots were fired. It was like listening to a record on a hifi with speakers on each side of the room – 'ba-boom.' Each gunshot sounded different, but the third shot fired was the loudest. I'm told Paige and Dr. Sinn pulled their triggers at the same time, hence the multiple sounds. Dr. Sinn's bullet missed Paige and struck the wall behind her. Paige's bullet would have hit me if it were not for Slayter's heroics. His momentum from pushing me placed Slayter where I had been standing. The bullet found Slayter. Eddie fired the third shot.

That one hit Paige in the chest, killing her instantly. There was blood splattered everywhere. It was awful."

Elizabeth took a moment to collect herself. "Weeks later," she continued, "an autopsy report on Paige revealed the poison pills she ingested would have finished her in minutes if Eddie's bullet hadn't killed her. In a sense, Eddie's shot was a mercy kill. Paige would have died in a fit of agony."

Holy wiped a hand over his mouth. He was trying to assimilate the scene as she painted it stroke by stroke. Earlier in the evening, Holy had asked her if she was pulling his leg by telling him a fictitious story. He was a believer now. Oh, how she wished it was fiction.

"I don't know what to say, Elizabeth." Holy shook his head. "If Officer Rose hadn't arrived, do you really believe Paige would have murdered you, Slayter, and Dr. Sinn in cold blood?"

"I don't have a sliver of doubt, Holy. That was Paige's intention the whole time, but she didn't have to worry about killing Dr. Sinn. He was found on the floor, dead from a massive heart attack. Eddie's theory was that with the three of us out of the way, all Paige needed to do was eliminate Doody, Rhoda, and probably Warren."

"You can count your lucky stars Officer Rose arrived when he did."

"We got lucky all right," she said. "But it was Doody who was the unsung hero. On his way to the police department after alerting Rhoda and Warren, he spotted Eddie helping a public works crew with a fallen tree in the road. Somehow, Doody persuaded Eddie that there was an even bigger emergency at Dr. Sinn's office."

"Certainly a crafty person like Paige would know she would be a prime suspect after the police found a slew of dead bodies."

"Back to Eddie's theory: before he showed up, Paige had a plan that would cover her murder tracks. With three dead bodies in the lab, she would have left Dr. Sinn's office to find Doody, Rhoda, and Warren and bring them back the same way she conned me. Once they were in the lab, she would have assassinated them – boom, boom, and boom."

"That still doesn't explain why Paige wouldn't be a suspect. Someone had to be the shooter. Plus Dr. Sinn must have kept notes at his office. Wouldn't Paige's name be in those notes?"

"Paige didn't smoke. Nor did she have a lighter. They found a full can of lighter fluid in her purse along with a box of wood matches. Eddie's take on it was that after Paige murdered everyone, either by the poisonous capsules or bullets, she would have set the doctor's office on fire, starting with the chemicals in his lab. It would have been difficult for the authorities to piece together what really happened in the charred remains."

"Then why did Paige take her own life?" Holy asked.

"Obviously, Paige was insane. How can you put yourself in a crazy person's head?" Elizabeth rubbed both arms. "Here's what I believe. Officer Eddie's presence put a major crimp in Paige's master plan. When he told her another squad car was coming, she must have panicked. She was facing going to prison for the rest of her life? Getting the electric chair? Having a shootout with the police? Or taking out her revenge on as many of the individuals who spoiled her grand plan as she could before dying?"

"Did the authorities investigate Paige's past? After all, she admitted to Slayter that she poisoned a chemist in his lab. How many more people did she kill?"

Elizabeth didn't answer Holy's question. A young man wearing a dark suit and tie entered the lounge and rushed to her table. Her heart hammered out excited beats as she stood to greet him. He took her in his arms and gave her a long and passionate kiss – the type that was socially unacceptable in a public place like Mr. B's. Yet for the indifferent loving couple, their spontaneous, affectionate behavior was more than appropriate.

"I should be angry." She stroked his cheek. "It's not like you to be so secretive. What were you doing in Oakland? It had to be an important meeting if you wore a suit and tie."

"It was the second most important meeting in my life. To answer your question, I was doing my darnedest to create a new chapter in our lives."

"What was the first most important meeting?" she asked.

"Meeting you, of course."

"Good answer." She put her arm through his arm and pointed to Holy. "I met an angel of a man while waiting for you. Holy, I'd like you to meet my fiancé, Slayter Jones."

"I was hoping it would be you." Holy shook Slayter's hand.

"I have no idea what *that* means." Slayter grinned. "It's nice to meet you, sir. Betsy said your name is Holy. What a curious name. Is that your given name? Or a nickname?"

Elizabeth and Holy exchanged smiles. Her annoyance with Slayter evaporated as soon as she saw him. Having him by her side was like a shot of adrenaline.

"Holy is my given name, Slayter."

Slayter sat down next to Elizabeth, took her hand into his, and invited Holy to their table.

She took several minutes to fill Slayter in on why she told a total stranger the story that had been festering inside for three years. He didn't interrupt or change expression. She wasn't sure if Slayter approved of her sharing the secret of their past.

"Holy, I can't thank you enough," Slayter said. "I don't know how you did it, but you got Betsy to talk about an experience that had her looking over her shoulder even when she was in a room by herself. It hasn't been easy for either one of us, especially Betsy. I found a way to rid the incident from my conscience by creating a writing project that dealt with my faults as well as what happened that Thanksgiving day in Bobsville. And I did it on my own without any help. It was cathartic. Now, maybe Betsy can do the same."

"If there was ever a couple who looked like they belong together, it's the two of you." Holy scooted his chair closer to the table. "I appreciate your kudos, Slayter, but it was really Sally, Dr. Sinn's grandniece and Paige's roommate, who prompted Elizabeth to open up. Now I see why Sally got so upset when she saw Elizabeth…I mean Betsy. She lost her great-uncle and a roommate. Does Sally also blame the other people involved?"

Elizabeth and Slayter nodded.

"I firmly believe fate brought all of us together for different reasons," Holy said. "If Sally hadn't confronted Elizabeth, I never would have learned about a certain Thanksgiving saga in Bobsville three years ago that kept me on the edge of my seat. What a story."

"If it wasn't for Holy, I would have left a long time ago." She pinched Slayter's arm.

"If I was a betting man, Elizabeth, I'd bet three dimes you would have stayed." Holy turned to Slayter. "You were wounded by Paige, but you look perfectly fit to me."

Slayter pointed to his ear. Then his other ear. The first ear he had pointed to was smaller and the upper part had a different patch of skin color. Then he lifted the hair next to the ear to reveal a scar.

"You mentioned fate," Slayter said. "A fraction of an inch and Paige would have gotten her wish. I don't know if the bullet or the fall knocked me out. I woke up in a hospital."

"Slayter must like you, Holy," Betsy said. "I've never seen him show anyone his scar." Her green eyes fixed on her fiancé. "Come on, Slayter, 'fess up. What's going on? Why were you at a meeting in Oakland wearing your suit? And why did you want me to meet you at Mr. B's?"

"I'll answer your last question first. Mr. B's is a perfect place to celebrate good news." Slayter leaned closer to her. "You're not going to believe this, Bets, but I was just offered a contract from a book publisher. They want to publish my novel. How cool is that?"

"Oh my God, why didn't you tell me you were meeting with a publisher?" Happy tears flowed down her cheeks as she hugged Slayter. "I can't believe it. I'm so proud of you."

"I kept the meeting a secret because I didn't want you to get your hopes up, only to be disappointed if there was no deal."

"Tell me everything," Elizabeth said, "How did this meeting even come about?"

"A small advertisement by a publisher in the *San Francisco Call Bulletin* Want Ads caught my eye. So I submitted the first three chapters along with a cover letter. Three weeks later, I received a letter from the publisher requesting the whole manuscript. I mailed the manuscript right away and waited almost four months for their response. Calling an agent or publisher is frowned upon in the literary world after a writer submits his work, so I waited patiently. When the days turned into weeks, then months, I figured they hated my story. Or worse yet, after my experience with Paige, maybe they were stealing it. Then I received a phone call from the publisher's managing editor. He wanted to meet with me to discuss the manuscript. When I was escorted into his office late this afternoon his greeting was, "Slayter Jones, we would like to publish your novel."

"Congratulations, Slayter," Holy said. "I'm assuming the manuscript you submitted to the publisher is *What If?*, the novel Paige wanted so badly."

"Ironically no, Holy. All of my submissions of *What If?* were rejected by agents and publishers. If Paige only knew. I finally shelved it and wrote another novel."

"I look forward to purchasing and reading your book. What is the title?"

"*Stuffed*. Based on a true story about an enabled man from a small town who had one hell of a Thanksgiving day. I believe you received a sneak preview of it from my fiancé."

"Does this mean you are going to quit your job and write novels full time?" Elizabeth asked, and then turned to Holy. "Slayter is a teaching golf pro at the Olympic Club Golf Course."

"Not until you receive the librarian position and I get the publisher's advance check."

Holy raised a hand until he got Brandi's attention. "I believe Champagne is in order. This is on me, Slayter. Actually, my brother is the liquor rep that sells Mr. B's most of their booze. Ordering a bottle of Champagne makes everybody happy, including my brother."

"That's very nice of you, Holy," Slayter said. "But it would be our pleasure to treat you as part of our celebration."

Elizabeth looked at Slayter as if he had lost his mind. Did he rob a bank before he got here? How embarrassing would it be if he was depending on her to help pay for it? She looked at her hands. Do they really make people wash dishes if a customer can't pay?

"What did you say to the managing editor, Slayter?" Holy asked.

"Where do I sign?" Slayter waited until they stopped laughing. "Actually, there was a lot of back and forth. They want to change a few things in my story. I was representing myself without an agent, which is probably not a good idea. So I told them I would like my attorney to look over the contract before I sign it." He eyed Holy. "Do you happen to know a really good literary attorney that you can recommend?"

"As a matter of fact, I do. One of my brothers is an attorney. He even represents several artists, including writers."

"How many brothers do you have? I'd love to hear what their names are." Slayter had to wait until they stopped giggling. "I don't understand the joke."

"I have seven brothers. Jim, Bill, Bob, Ken, John, Tom, and Fred," Holy answered. "We are laughing because Elizabeth asked me the same question."

"Not only that," Elizabeth added, "Holy promised to buy us dinner if I could guess his last name. He says it goes well with his first name."

Brandi placed three Champagne glasses on the table. She popped the cork and poured, then placed the bottle in an ice bucket. They raised their glasses to do the clinking bit.

"Here's to new friends," Holy said. "I wish you both great health, success in your careers, and happiness together in marriage, like the one I had with my dear Margaret." Holy sipped, then placed his glass on the table. "I have one last question for you, Slayter. Did you make good on your promise to eliminate Eddie Rose's 'Goat' moniker?"

"I did," Slayter said. "The following spring, I set up a team reunion at the Bobsville High School football field to reenact that last play again. Most of the original team was on the field. Family and friends were in the stands. The stadium clock was set to show five seconds left in the game. We broke the huddle and went into the same formation. I barked out signals, took the snap from the center, faded back to pass, pumped a fake to Rudy, and lobbed a pass to Eddie in the end zone. Guess what? Eddie dropped the ball again. The whole team fell down laughing. Boos and jeers came from the stands. Eddie complained the pass was too soft. I got everyone to huddle up again. We ran the same play as before. This time, Eddie caught the ball. There was a thunderous cheer from the crowd. Eddie was carried off the field on his teammate's shoulders as a hero."

"What a wonderful way to resolve that issue." Holy reached into his coat pocket and removed a handful of business cards. He thumbed through them until he found the right one and handed it to Slayter. "This is my brother Tom's business card. The law firm he works for is here in the city. I'll talk to Thomas tomorrow over turkey. Make sure to tell him I sent you."

"Thank you, Holy." Slayter glanced at the black print on glossy white stock card.

"Thomas Samoli, Attorney at Law."

"Holy Samoli," Elizabeth belted out. "You are Holy Samoli."

"Samoli is my last name," Holy said, with a sly smile. He nodded to Brandi. "And the two of you are my guests for dinner."

Moments later, the hostess in the long green gown and stiletto heels entered the cocktail lounge and approached Holy.

"Sir, your table for three is ready." She led them into the dining area and waited for each member of the party to be seated. "As usual, your server tonight will be Dylan. Enjoy your dinners."

"Good evening, Mr. Samoli and guests." The tuxedoed waiter handed out menus. "My name is Dylan, and I will be taking your orders. Before I introduce tonight's entrees, I highly recommend our special appetizer that comes with an unbelievable tangy mustard sauce dip - oven-roasted, crispy Brussels sprouts. They are something to die for."

–THE END–

ACKNOWLEDGEMENTS

Without special assistance from Martha Clark Scala (Author of *Assembling a Life: Claiming the Artist in My Father & Myself*), Debby Rose and Joanne Davis, this novel never would have come to life.

A heartfelt thank you to the following people for contributing, in a myriad of ways, to my novels *The Ticker, Will to Kill, When the Enemy Is You, The Crackerjack,* and *Stuffed – Thanksgiving Will Never Be the Same.*

Debbie Aldred, Fred Aldred, Allison Anson, Ava Archibald, Bill Archibald, Bob Archibald, Julie Archibald, Nancy Archibald, Frank Baldwin (Author of *Balling the Jack & Jake & Mimi)*Alyn Beals, Scott Benner (Mayor of Bennerville), Robert Berry (Soundtek Studios),Elaine Blossom, Randal Brandt (The Bancroft Library at the University of California, Berkeley), Donna Smith Brown, Bill Burns, Barbara Butera, Frank Butera, Dennis Cacace, Carole Carl, Sharyl Carter, Danielle Carvalhaes, Sue Chamberlain, Shiela Cockshott, Carroll Collins III, Mary Ruth Conley, Al Connell, Georgia Corneliusen, Raquel Cosare, Ryan Cosare, Diana Crosetti, Pat Cuendet (Author of *The Ghost In The Garden)*, Brian A. Davis (Host of *Damn Good Movie Memories* - The Podcast & That Metal Station -*The Bad Beat*), Darryl Davis, Gary Davis, Chris Deners, Helen Dolan, Barbara Drotar (Author of *Searching For Sophia*), Allison Evens, Rob Evens, Gin Geraldi, Joni Gimnicher, Steve Gimnicher, Sue Goldman, Jeannie Graham, Margi Grant, Karen Griffiths, Mary Garon, Barbara Hembey, Bill Hembey, Carol Henderson, Laurel Anne Hill (Author of *Heroes Arise & The Engine Woman's Light)*, Jen Ingalls, Leslie Jimenez, Ray Johnson, Warren Joiner, Mark Jones, Murray Kanefsky, Marie Kennedy, Natalie Korman (Copy Editor), Julie Kosmides, Naty Kwan, Garrett Lee, Becky Levine, Jennifer Lindsey, Kathy Love, Dr. Mike Ludovico, Serena Ludovico, Laura Lujan, Jacqueline Machado, Karin Marshall, Mike Marshall, Cliff Martin, Betty Martin, Alicia Mazzoni, Jana McBurney-Lin (Author of *My Half of the Sky & Blossoms & Bayonets*),

Sharen McConnell, Lorraine McGrath, Rockin' Roy McKinney, Tracy McNamara, Amanda McTigue (Author of *Going to Solace*), Princess Kristina Merlini, Virginia Messer, Kristol Miles, Gus Milon, Kathleen Moore, Jeff Morena, Sue Murray, Colleen Conley Navarro, Dr. David Nichols, Bill Orrock, Jasmine Partida, Beverly Paterson, Alicia Robertson (Robertson Publishing), Ken Rolandelli, Lora Rolandelli, Teresa LeYung Ryan (Author of *Love Made of Heart)*, Seton Hospital Wound Care Staff, Elaine Silver (Story Editor extraordinaire), Scott Smith (Author of *The Ruins & A Simple Plan*), Dr. Kalpanu Srinivasan, Steve Stahl, Dr. Lisa Stiller, Roseanne Strahle, Dylan Stratinsky, Kelli Jo Stratinsky, Pam Tavernier, Rick Taylor, SchcrrieTaylor, Scott Taylor, Steve Teani, Catherine Teitelbaum, Gail Tesi, Joanne Thoorsell, Elizabeth Tuck, Bill Tyler, Marge Tyree, Pat Vitucci, Leslie Walsh, Vicki Williams, Bob Young, Rebecca Young, Donnalyn Zarzeczny, Joe Zukin.

*My apologies, in advance, if I omitted a deserving person's name.